MW01529318

By The Book

Alex McGilvery

Cover Illustration
by Danita Stallard

Copyright Alex McGilvery 2014
ISBN 978-1-329-08367-7

Celtic Frog Publishing

This is a work of fiction. Names, characters, businesses, places, events and incidents are either the products of the author's imagination or used in a fictitious manner. Any resemblance to actual persons, living or dead, or actual events is purely coincidental.

Chapter 1

Paul didn't notice that God came to visit because he was concentrating on fixing breakfast according to the Book. It was Tuesday, that's why he made oatmeal. He used exactly the prescribed single measure, stirred carefully to avoid lumps as it cooked to just barely thick enough to stand a spoon in. He scraped the glutenous mess into his bowl and poured in the proper measure of milk.

Only as he started to eat, did he notice God waiting patiently in the doorway. Paul had heard of such things before. His great-grandfather Enoch claimed to walk with God on a daily basis. Paul had to make do with the Book. He flipped the immense leather bound volume open to the "Visitation by God" page marked by a yellow bookmark and began to follow the instructions.

"Welcome, O God," he said. His voice didn't quiver at all, though his heart raced in his chest. "Tell what I may do so you will not be displeased with your servant." An odd expression crossed God's face, but Paul didn't quite catch it since he was reading the next instruction in the Book.

"Please," Paul said, "Sit and join me at my feast." A bowl of rapidly cooling oatmeal and milk didn't seem like much of a feast, but it was the breakfast for Tuesday. God had to be pleased with how well he was following the Book.

God sighed and sat across from him.

"No thanks," God said. "I never cared for oatmeal. Go ahead and eat."

Paul sighed and started spooning the oatmeal into his mouth. Since it counted as a soft food he was only required to chew it ten times. He didn't much like oatmeal either, but what else would you eat on Tuesday?. Somehow, having God watch him eat made the oatmeal even more tasteless.

When he had finished breakfast, he looked up to see if God was still there. He was. He didn't look much like Paul expected.

God should be immense and powerful, much too big to fit in Paul's humble kitchen. But here he was dressed in a dusty robe and not shining at all. In fact he appeared a little tired.

"What do you require of me?" Paul asked after looking in his Book again. Why the question changed from one asking to the next didn't bother Paul. It was in the Book. As long as he followed the Book, God wouldn't be displeased with him.

"You are going to go on a quest," God said. "There are some things that I need you to find for me."

"A quest?" Paul flipped through the Book. He knew the Book as well as anyone and he'd never read anything about a quest. "What's a quest?" he asked finally, "And how do I do it?"

"A quest is a special kind of journey," God said. Paul thought there might be a slight edge of irritation in God's voice. He felt the oatmeal sit like a lump in his stomach. He was displeasing God! In a moment God would smite him with a lightning bolt, or maybe fire and brimstone.

"Relax, Paul," God said, "I need you to go on this quest. I'm not going to smite you."

Paul tried to relax, but he was sure he wasn't doing very well at it. He turned to the Book, maybe there was something on relaxing there. God, very gently, reached over and closed the Book.

"Some things are not in the Book," God said. He sounded sad. Paul wasn't sure he wanted to know what kind of things would make God sad. "I will teach you what you need to learn. You are to take a companion on the journey."

"How will I know who to take?" Paul asked. "I wouldn't want to take the wrong person."

"You will take the first person you meet today as your companion. The two of you will share the quest and learn from each other." He stood up and Paul was sure he was going to leave. There was something that he needed to do when God left. He was sure of it, but God had closed the Book, and Paul did not plan to open the book that God shut.

"I will do all that you ask of me, O God."

"I'm sure you will," God said. "Open the Book, Paul."

Paul opened the Book to the place with the yellow bookmark and found a blank page. He turned to another page and it was blank too, so was the next, and the next after that. The entire Book was blank! He looked at God.

"How will I know how to please you if I don't have the Book?" This time his voice quivered.

"Tear a page out of the Book, Paul."

Paul reached out with trembling hands and tore a page out of the Book. God reached over and touched the paper with a finger.

"When you need guidance," God said, "it will direct you." Paul looked at him and for a moment he saw something vaster than anything he had ever imagined. Then God had gone, and he stood alone in his kitchen. He looked down at the page in his hand.

Sit down and take a few deep breaths

Paul hadn't realized he was standing. He sat carefully in his chair and took a deep breath, then another. How many was a few? Three, four?

Keep breathing

Paul sat on his chair and breathed until he stopped shaking.

Do Tuesday

Paul got up and washed his bowl and spoon, carefully wiping them each three times. He washed the pot too and set it upside down on the stove. Once he finished it was time for him to go and look after his garden. He meticulously weeded the small plot of land that grew most of what he ate. The feel and smell of the dirt almost made him forget about God's visit and the quest. There were peas and lettuce and even a tomato that were ripe. He picked them and carried his harvest into the kitchen. When he completed the weeding he went out to the pasture to look after his sheep. The ewe provided him with fleece to trade and milk for his oatmeal. It wasn't time to sheer her, but he milked her and put the milk aside while he made sure that she was healthy and uninjured.

First he examined her head and eyes. His fingers travelled down her neck, then down each leg. He lifted each foot in sequence to check her feet. Then he checked her back and stomach, then hind legs and feet. She smelled like she was supposed to - earthy and like wet wool. The ewe simply stood and chewed at some grass. She was used to this. Paul did it every Tuesday.

After he checked his ewe, he made a count of the other sheep in the pasture. There were fourteen. All was well. He picked up the milk and started walking back to his home. God said that he was to take the first person he met. Maybe it would be Diana! She would have to come with him. It would be a long and dangerous journey and they would have to become close companions. She might even learn to like him. Paul was lost in his daydream when he heard a voice hail him.

"Hey, Paul!" The voice that wasn't Diana's yanked him from his pleasant dreams. Daniel jogged up to him. "I need some vegetables." He hoisted a bag. "I have eggs."

"Come to the house," Paul said in a despondent voice. He saw Daniel give him an odd look.

"It is Tuesday, isn't it?"

"Of course it is. What else could it be?"

"So, we always trade on Tuesday," Daniel said. "You're looking at me like it was Friday."

"How could Tuesday be Friday?" Paul said.

"But you like Friday much more than Tuesday, don't you?" Daniel swung the bag with the eggs. "Fridays are when you see Diana. I get the feeling that you like her cheese a lot more than you like my eggs."

"I follow the Book," Paul said and walked a little faster.

"Of course you do," Daniel said. "Don't we all?"

"Lo, the man and the woman looked at the tree," Paul said in his Book quoting voice "and saw that the fruit was good, but God had said not to eat of the fruit of the Tree and so the man and the woman refrained. They went to God in the cool of the evening and asked God to tell them what to do next. They feared to displease him. God told them to be fruitful and enjoy life, but the man and the woman insisted that God tell them what they should do so that they wouldn't offend God by chance. In the morning and in the evening they asked God the same question. Each evening and each morning God told them to be fruitful and enjoy life. But still the man and the woman feared to offend God. So God gave them the Book."

"You don't need to quote scripture at me," Daniel said. "I have my own copy of the Book."

"Sorry," Paul said. Of course Daniel had his own copy and would know it as well as he did. Didn't every person find the Book when they were old enough to read? No one knew where they came from, even the Book said little about the Book. Each person's Book was subtly different. Paul's Book made him a gardener and shepherd while Daniel's Book made him raise chickens.

Paul wondered briefly if Daniel's Book said the same things about welcoming God as Paul's did. He was sure it did. All the Books came with that yellow marker so they could turn to it as soon as God appeared. It was just that God didn't show up very often.

They reached Paul's home and went inside. Daniel went to the vegetables and began picking out what he wanted. Paul looked at the Page. He was already thinking of it in the capitals he usually reserved for the Book.

Tell him

"Uh, Daniel," Paul said. Daniel turned and looked at him. How was Paul supposed to tell him that he was supposed to be Paul's companion on the quest? What if he didn't believe him? He peeked at The Page.

Tell him

"I'm going on a quest." Paul said.

"What's a quest?" Daniel asked.

"It is a special journey that God is sending me on."

"I've never heard of a quest in the Book before."

"It isn't in the Book," Paul said. "God came for breakfast and told me to go."

"Of course he did," Daniel said and rolled his eyes, "and he ate oatmeal with you."

"He doesn't like oatmeal."

"Who does?" Daniel said.

That was strange, Paul thought, because it was true. Not many people liked oatmeal. Yet everybody ate oatmeal on Tuesday.

TELL HIM

Oops, he was getting The Page angry.

"You're supposed to come."

"For breakfast?" Daniel frowned, "I don't want to eat oatmeal twice."

"No," Paul said. He took a deep breath. He wondered if God had felt frustrated like this. "You are supposed to be my companion on my quest."

"Really?"

"Really," Paul said. "Come and see."

Daniel walked over to the big book and flipped it open. His eyes widened when he saw that it was blank.

"What happened to your Book?"

"God gave me this for the quest," Paul said and showed him the page.

Daniel, you will go with Paul.

"I guess that's it," Daniel said. "But what am I supposed to do to get ready?"

Pack one bag. Put one set of extra clothes in. Pack food for a week. Wear your cloak.

"I'm off to pack," Daniel said. He waved the vegetables at Paul. "These good?"

"Sure," Paul said. He didn't watch Daniel leave. He pulled out a few bags.

Take the strongest. Leave space for some cheese.

Paul decided the strongest was the next to biggest bag. He looked at the page, but it hadn't changed. Rolling up his spare clothes as tight as he could get them, he stuffed them in the bag. Then carefully measured out the food for the week, and packed it too. His sheepskin cloak was heavy, but it was a familiar weight on his shoulders. There was space for cheese.

"What's going to happen to my home and my garden and my sheep?" Paul asked as he hefted the bag.

Go get your cheese. Give everything but your bag to the first person you meet.

Paul shrugged. If the Page said so. He was going to miss his things though. He put the bag over his shoulder and headed off toward Diana's. In his free hand he carried the vegetables and eggs that he hadn't packed.

It was odd how the familiar path suddenly became charged with meaning. He noted each landmark, each stone or root. He wouldn't be passing this way again, or at least not soon. Yet even as he nodded at each turn in the path, his heart was pounding with excitement. God had come to him!

He rounded the last bend before Diana's father's house and almost bumped into Zaccheus. He wondered why the richest man in town needed his home and sheep, but that's what the Page said.

"Zaccheus," Paul said, and the fat man turned to look at him. Paul had never had much reason to talk to Zaccheus before. He wondered how the man could get fat on oatmeal on Tuesdays. "Zaccheus, I am going on a quest. the Book told me to give everything I own to you."

Zaccheus smiled. "I will look after it well," he said. "You must be truly blessed to be sent on a quest."

"My ewe gets checked for injury or disease every Tuesday," Paul said, "and the garden needs weeding every morning."

"I will ensure that all is done."

"You must care for my things yourself," Paul said. "I am giving them to you, not to your servants."

"Do you not trust the Book?" Zaccheus frowned at Paul.

"Yes, of course." Paul thought of his Book, sitting blank in his kitchen.

"Then trust me to follow my Book to care for your property. God would not give it to someone who would not do the right things."

"Yes, of course," Paul said, "but..." The page in his hand rustled and he looked at it.

Go get cheese.

"What is that?" Zaccheus pointed at the Page.

"It is what God gave to me to guide me on my quest."

"God gave it to you?" Zaccheus reached for the page. Paul reluctantly let him take it. The Books were the final arbiters of any conflict. This wasn't really a conflict, and it wasn't quite a Book any more, but it was the way things were. Zaccheus looked at the page and went pale. He pushed it back into Paul's hands and went up the path almost at a run.

Paul looked at the page and wondered what it had said to upset Zaccheus so much. What he read was

Cheese.

Paul didn't know why the cheese was so important, but he was glad enough to see Diana. He hurried down the path. Now that he owned nothing but what he carried, the bag on his shoulder felt very light.

Diana lived with her father. They made cheese from milk they traded for. The only thing that Paul liked more than the cheese was Diana. When she came to the door Paul couldn't help staring at her one last time. She was only slightly shorter than he was, but he was sure she was just as strong. In spite of her strength she looked soft and curvaceous. Her hair braided fell to her waist. She frowned at Paul.

"It's Tuesday," she said.

"I'm going on a quest," Paul said. "I need cheese."

"Come in," she said. As he walked into her home he saw her go to her Book and flip it open. Whatever it said made her gasp and put her hand to her mouth. Paul wondered if being sent on a quest was such a blessing after all.

"Come," Diana said and led him to the cool, dark room where the cheeses were stored.

Paul put the bag with the vegetables and eggs on the table and his sack on the floor then followed her. In the room she picked up a small round of cheese and wrapped it in a cloth then handed it to Paul. He packed it carefully in his pack. This was the last thing he needed before he left. He thought he'd go over to Daniel's and make sure his companion was ready.

Paul was unprepared for Diana to throw her arms around him and kiss him, but he made the best of it, trying to lock the memory into his head so he could bring it out to think about while he traveled.

"The Book said to kiss you goodbye if I ever wanted to see you again," Diana said into his shoulder. Paul felt something in him relax. He would live. He'd come back and see Diana again.

"Did it say just one kiss?" he asked. She looked up at him with a smile.

"No," she said. The second kiss was even better than the first. Paul let his sack drop to the floor so he could use both arms to hold her.

"I hope you didn't crack the eggs." Daniel leaned against the doorpost of Diana's home. He held a stack with one hand. Diana stepped back. She was still smiling, but tears were running down her face too.

Paul picked up his sack.

"Goodbye," he said.

"You have to come back now," Diana said.

"The Book will guide me," Paul said, "and you as well."

He walked out of the house and he could hear Daniel following him.

"The Book didn't arrange for me to get any farewell kisses," Daniel said, but he sounded more amused than jealous.

"God has his reasons," Paul said. "Maybe that was to make up for giving all my possessions to Zaccheus."

"You had to give away your house and everything?" Daniel said. "My neighbour is looking after my chickens. I left my book open to the right page."

"You aren't bringing your Book?"

"Are you kidding? It weighs a ton. It didn't say to pack it, so I didn't."

"How will you know what to do?" Paul said. "You need your Book so you don't displease God."

"You have the Page," Daniel said. "It will do for both of us."

Paul looked at the Page.

Keep walking.

For the first time in his life, Paul left Eben, his home.

Chapter 2

They walked on the path away from their home. Paul knew that the next village was two or three days journey. He thought its name was Cepha, but the Book had never sent him there.

At first the quest was exciting. Paul saw new scenery with every step. The tang of the dust on his mouth tasted like adventure. Birds sang and flitted through the trees. The sun shone warm, and the breeze blew cool. The only thing that would have made it better would have been Diana's warm hand in his. Paul smiled and let himself remember the kiss. He thought about the feel of her soft body against his.

"Just how far are we supposed to walk?" Daniel came back to where Paul stood daydreaming.

"I don't know," Paul said. "The Page just says to keep walking."

"Helpful," Daniel said. "Try to keep the pace up while you are mooning over Diana, or we'll never get there."

Paul started to get angry, but he saw the grin on Daniel's face. His companion was taking the fact that Paul got the kiss and he didn't with good humour.

"I will try," Paul said and grinned back at Daniel. Daniel slapped him on the shoulder and they started walking again.

"What do you think this is all about?"

"I don't know," Paul said. "I haven't really thought about it."

"God visits you, turns your life upside down, makes sure you get a good kiss goodbye, and you don't think about it?"

"I don't think much at all," Paul said. "Everything is in the Book."

"So you never wonder why?"

"Why what?"

"Why anything?" Daniel started waving the arm that wasn't carrying his bag in the air. "Why do chickens need gravel to eat? Why is Zaccheus so fat? Why are we here?"

"The Book..."

"Not everything is in the Book, Paul."

"God said the same thing," Paul said. "He sounded sad."

"What would make God sad?"

"If we displease him," Paul said. "But we are doing what we are told." He shrugged and switched the bag to the other shoulder. "I don't know, Daniel. I'm sure we'll find out when we need to."

The sun rose higher into the sky and the day got warmer. The breeze faded and died. Flies buzzed around their heads. Sometimes they landed and bit through Paul's shirt. He sweated under his heavy cloak, and the flies stuck to the moisture on his face. The bag that had seemed so light when he was talking with Zaccheus started feeling heavier and heavier. Paul switched it from one shoulder to the other and back. It didn't get any lighter. Paul's mouth tasted like the dust which coated his teeth and made him thirsty. They walked through the day. Sometimes they talked about what they saw, but mostly they just walked.

When the sun went down behind the trees the shade was a relief. Daniel saw a tiny spring beside the path and they drank their fill of water. It was the most delicious water Paul had ever had.

The cool of the shade became the chill of night as they reached a clearing in the woods. Paul heard a stream running close by.

"Let's stop here for the night," Daniel said.

Paul took out the page.

Stop

"OK," he said and let his bag down to the ground. It was Tuesday, so Paul pulled out the lentils and some greens from his garden.

"What are you going to cook them in?" Daniel asked.

"I..." Paul looked at the food in his hand. He supposed they could eat the greens raw, but...

"I'll go get some water," Daniel said hefting a pot. "It's a good thing that we both didn't need to pack a cheese along."

Paul measured the lentils into the pot and they let them sit while they built a fire. Daniel had brought the flint and steel too. Maybe there was an advantage to this thinking thing. It would have been better if the Page had told him to bring the pot and fire starter. Of course, there wouldn't have been room for the cheese, and he wouldn't have had to go see Diana.

Daniel put a bowl of lentils and greens into Paul's hands.

"I'll eat out of the pot," Daniel said. "I only brought one bowl."

"Thanks, Daniel," Paul said. Tuesday wasn't his favourite meal, but this was the best Tuesday he'd ever eaten.

He tried to sleep wrapped up in his cloak. The night was chilly enough that he was happy to have the heavy cloak. He heard Daniel tossing and turning. Daniel's cloak was a lighter woven cloak. Easier in the heat of day, but not as warm at night.

"Daniel," Paul said, "come, put your back against mine and share my cloak."

"Thanks," Daniel said. They lay back to back and soon their combined heat made them comfortable enough to sleep.

The birds woke them in the morning. Daniel got to his feet with a groan. He stretched until Paul heard his joints pop. When Paul tried to stand he understood the groan. His mattress at home wasn't very thick, but it was much softer than the ground.

"I'll get the water," he said to Daniel, "if you get the bread out of my bag." By the time he got back with the water, Daniel was toasting the bread on the fire. He handed the sticks to Paul and dug into his backpack. He pulled out a tiny pot.

"The Book led me to some honey the other day," Daniel said, and Paul's mouth watered. Honey was a rare treat. They spread some on the toast and ate every sweet crumb. Paul licked his fingers and sighed.

"That was a really good Wednesday."

Daniel shrugged and packed up the pot carefully. They drank their fill of the water, then Daniel put that pot away too.

"We'd better get going," he said. "Let's see how far we can get before it warms up too much."

They walked along the path. It started winding uphill, and the trees changed. They had larger leaves than the trees at home and they cast a green shade over the path. Rocks poked through the path and Paul had to watch to make sure he didn't trip. The walking worked out the stiffness from the night and soon he was pleasantly warm. Daniel pointed ahead in silence, and Paul saw a deer in the woods. It looked at him then walked away.

Walking uphill tired him out quickly. His legs burned as he took each step. He'd never hurt so much in his life.. There were more springs though, and the air was cooler. The cloak didn't make it as overwhelmingly warm as the day before.

They camped under some trees that were covered with soft needles instead of leaves. Paul breathed in deeply. The smell of the strange trees was sharp, but pleasant and the fallen needles made the ground almost as soft as Paul's mattress. The night was colder, and he was glad for the heat of Daniel's back against his.

In the morning Paul got up first and filled the pot with water. It was Thursday, oatmeal again. He thought of the honey from yesterday and sighed wistfully. When the water boiled he put two measures of oats into the pot and stirred it carefully.

When it was ready he put Daniel's portion in his bowl and handed it to him. There was no milk because Paul couldn't think of how to carry it. He hoped Zaccheus enjoyed it before it went bad.

If oatmeal was unpleasant, oatmeal without milk was worse. Daniel reached into his bag and pulled out the honey.

"We aren't to sweeten the oatmeal," Paul said. "The Book says to eat it with milk."

"It doesn't forbid honey," Daniel said. He put a large dollop on the mess in his bowl. "We don't have any milk."

"But we can't go against the Book," Paul said. "We'll displease God."

"I can't imagine God being displeased by a little honey."

Paul remembered God saying that he didn't care for oatmeal. Maybe it was because he didn't put honey on it. He looked around fearfully. Surely God would come and smite him for such impious thoughts. Nothing happened. Daniel sat and ate his honeyed oatmeal as the birds sang and the sun shone.

"God chose me to be your companion," Daniel said. "If you don't trust me, you have to trust God."

"OK then," Paul said and held out the pot. Daniel put a dollop of honey on Paul's oatmeal.

"This is the only way I can stand to eat the stuff," Daniel said.

Paul wondered how often Daniel put honey on his oatmeal, but the sweet taste of the honey distracted him. It tasted oddly like Diana's lips. Before he realized, Paul was scraping the last of the oatmeal from the bottom of the pot. They washed their dishes in the stream before Daniel packed them away.

"I think God must have chosen you as my companion because of your wisdom," Paul said. "I had hoped to meet Diana first."

"That would have made your journey much more interesting," Daniel said, "especially the nights." He grinned at Paul and Paul's heart lifted. He wasn't Diana, but maybe Daniel was going to be a good companion in his own way.

They walked along. The path still was mostly uphill, and the trees with the soft needles became the most common. Some darker trees with harsher needles appeared and Paul hoped he didn't need to sleep on those needles.

They arrived at Cepha in the middle of the afternoon. It was a larger village than Paul's home. A herd of cattle grazed in one pasture and sheep in another. People were hoeing an entire field of vegetables. Paul and Daniel walked into the centre of the village where there were some people sitting behind booths filled with all kinds of goods. After the quiet of the walk, Paul's ears ached with the sound of so many people talking at once.

"Maybe we should stop and trade for another bowl," Daniel said, "and perhaps a skin for water."

"What do we have to trade?"

"You have a cheese, don't you?" Daniel said.

"I thought we were going to eat it."

"A whole cheese?"

"Diana gave it to me."

"She also gave you a kiss, and the kiss is lighter."

Paul sighed, and they found a man sitting at a table covered with bowls and other things.

"We'd like to trade for a bowl and maybe some water skins," Paul said.

"What do you have to trade?" the man asked. Paul pulled the cheese out of his bag.

"I don't need any cheese," the man said. He waved at someone across the square and a woman walked across.

"What you have here, Levi?"

"This boy has a cheese," Levi said.

The woman took the cheese and hefted it. She smelled it and even sniffed at it.

"It looks like a fine cheese," she said. "It's more aged than what I make. I'll give you ten for it."

Paul wondered, ten what? He looked at Daniel, but his companion just lifted an eyebrow. Paul looked at his Page.

Ask for twenty.

"I'd like twenty," Paul said, still not knowing what he was asking for.

"Hmm." The woman stared into the distance for a moment, then sniffed the cheese again. "The Book might let me give you twelve."

Paul glanced at the Page.

Fifteen.

"Fifteen," he said.

The woman sighed, "May I not displease God, fourteen."

Take it.

"I'll take it," Paul said. The woman put the cheese down on the table for a moment while she pulled out a tiny bag. She carefully counted out fourteen little round objects and handed them to Paul.

"It's money," she said to Paul. "You can trade these for anything in the market, if you have enough of them." She hoisted the cheese.

"May the Book give you good trading, Levi."

"You too, Tamara," Levi said. He looked at Paul and smiled. "Now what did you want to buy?"

With the help of the Page, Paul bought a small bowl and tiny knife. He even had a few coins left. That was what Levi called the objects. It seemed strange to be discussing such tiny things with such seriousness, but Daniel told him it made sense to do it this way. They spent the last of their coins on a pack that had straps to go over the shoulder. It was big enough to hold most of their stuff. The man that sold it to them said that it would soon enough hold all of it.

"There are two roads out of here," the man said. He showed them how to stow their gear so the pack wouldn't have hard bulges to stick into their back. "The road west will take you to a river in four days. There's a large town called Brurn on its banks. Ask the Book to send you there. The road to the north leads to death.

"How do you know that?" Daniel asked.

"The Book hasn't sent anyone there in years."

Paul looked at the Page.

North

"Well, God wouldn't have sent us on this quest just to let us die," Daniel said.

"Diana kissed me," Paul said. "She said her Book told her to kiss me if she wanted to see me again."

"Well then, north it is."

"May your Book be kind to you," the man said and turned away to talk to someone else.

They walked through the square and out the other side. The narrow path they had been following had become road. In the distance, high mountains lifted up into the clouds. The road was wide and straight, but it looked like no one used it. Weeds grew up in the centre of the road and where it entered the forest Paul could see a tree lying across it.

"Well," Daniel said, "God must know what she is doing."

Chapter 3

The road wasn't as pleasant walking as the path had been. The surface was gravel that slipped and crunched under their feet. It didn't wind around obstacles, but cut through them. Paul marveled at the effort it must have taken to cut through the hills. Still, it steadily climbed as they walked.

"Did he say how far we had to travel to the north?" Daniel asked.

"No," Paul said. "It is four days west to the River, but all he said about north was don't go there."

"I was just wondering if we have enough food."

"Why would you think about that?"

"He said all our stuff would fit in the pack soon enough. I was trying to decide what he meant. As we eat our food it will take up less space."

"I didn't consider that." Paul felt the weight of the pack on his back. "It feels heavy enough now."

"Let's hope it stays that way long enough to get us where we are going."

"God wouldn't let us starve."

"I wonder how long we can go without food?"

"I'm pretty sure I don't want to find out."

They walked in silence for a while. The trees loomed over the road and brush made a in impenetrable fence. There was no clearing for them to camp so they huddled at the side of the road when it got dark. Paul didn't object when Daniel made their meal with a scant measure. It was colder that night, and even with the shared heat under the sheepskin cloak Paul shivered through the night.

The forest they walked through the next day was dark and gloomy. Trees with hard spiky needles surrounded them. Black birds flew through the trees called harshly. All around them moss draped from dead looking branches and carpeted the forest floor.

Every once in a while they had to fight their way through a tree that had fallen across the road. The trees seemed to be getting bigger. At first they just had to push through branches that snapped easily but made Paul's hands sticky with sap. It didn't wash off with water and made his skin itch. By afternoon they had to climb and weave their way through branches that were as thick as smaller trees or hoist themselves up and over trunks that lay like walls across the road. Their clothes were covered with sticky spots and needles from the trees.

The light had almost gone when they came up against a massive fallen tree Even with Daniel standing on Paul's shoulders they couldn't reach the top of the trunk.

"We'd better stop here for the night and have a look at it in the morning," Daniel said. "We can light a fire and keep a little warmer."

It didn't take long for them to find plenty of dry wood and soon they had a little fire going. The warmth it gave was as much from its cheery light as the heat of the wood. Daniel poured water into the pot. The fire snapped and popped at them, but it heated the water quickly enough.

"That's the last of our water. We'll have to find more tomorrow before we eat breakfast."

They ate their scant dinner, then rolled up in the cloaks under the curve of the huge tree trunk.

Rain woke Paul in the middle of the night. The tree mostly sheltered them, but he set out the pot to gather the water from the rain. Even with the rain not soaking them directly the air was damp and cold. It took a long time for him to fall back to sleep.

When they woke in the morning the fire was out and the wood was soaked. None of Daniel's efforts could get the fire going again.

"We should have bread instead of oatmeal," Daniel said.

"But it is an oatmeal day," Paul said. "Isn't it?"

"I think so, but I'm not sure we can make oatmeal without a fire."

"But..." Paul sighed. "You're right, but it feels strange not eating oatmeal on oatmeal days."

"You'll get used to it."

"What?"

"I never liked oatmeal," Daniel said. "I usually eat bread."

"But the Book says to eat oatmeal on Tuesday, Thursday and Saturday. It is very clear on that."

"I put oats in my bread dough," Daniel said. "I think that makes it OK." He shrugged as he put a dollop of honey on each slice of bread. "God hasn't smitten me for it."

"That sounds an awful lot like being a Chooser!"

"Are you going to put me to death then?" Daniel said. "That's what every Book says to do with a Chooser. Would God have sent you out with a Chooser?"

"I guess not." Paul took his slice of bread and honey from Daniel. It tasted sweeter somehow, maybe because it wasn't in the Book. "I wonder why God tells us to eat oatmeal when even God doesn't like it much.

"Who knows?"

They finished their meagre breakfast in silence. Paul looked at the water in the pot. It looked green. He thought about eating green oatmeal and shuddered. He poured the water out and packed the pot.

"Let's go," he said. "It's not going to get any drier."

They fought their way west along the trunk. The rain chilled Paul's head as it slicked his hair. Cold drips ran down the back of his neck. The forest ran with water and their clothes clung to them and pulled heat from their bodies. Wet clothes chaffed them in uncomfortable places. Even the sheepskin cloak wasn't impervious to the deluge. It weighed Paul down like the full pack had, but with no promise of food. They took most of the morning to reach the place where the tree had torn itself from the forest floor. Paul looked nervously down into the hole the tree had left. He saw just a glint of a reflection from the bottom. The wet earth wouldn't be easy to climb. They made sure to stay well back from the edge.

Once around the hole they had to fight their way back to the road. There was a little more space on the north side of the tree and they were able to hug the massive trunk and make better time.

"Well that was a good morning's work," Daniel said. "We took half the day to travel fifteen feet." He grunted and pushed away from the tree. "Let's hope there aren't any more this size. He walked off down the road. Paul followed. The combined weight of the wet sheepskin cloak and the pack made him stumble a little.

The rain lasted all that day. They had no fire at supper either. Daniel gave them extra bread.

"It's going to go to mold in this wet anyway," he said, "I'd rather eat the bread than throw it away."

The rain continued all night. Paul didn't argue when Daniel again handed him extra slices. He was shivering too much to talk.

They walked through the rain for two more days. Daniel had to pick mold off the bread before he sliced it. The last day there was more mold than bread and he threw the remains away.

"That was the last of it." Daniel said, "We didn't do too bad. We'll need a fire tonight or we'll be chewing dry oats."

They didn't eat dry oats that next morning, but only because the mold had gotten into the oats and turned them green. Instead, Daniel used the little knife to poke a hole in the eggs and they ate raw eggs for breakfast. It was disgusting, but it was food.

The rain stopped that day and the temperature plummeted. Their wet clothes stuck to them sucking the heat from their bodies.

"We'll have to get a fire going," Daniel said, "or the cold will kill us."

The pack held everything they owned and still it hung mostly empty on Paul's back. They pushed on. Paul looked at the Page.

Keep walking.

"Not terribly helpful," Daniel muttered.

Soon after that Paul fell to the road. He pushed himself to his feet, but Daniel had to help him walk. Paul didn't think Daniel was in much better shape. They were stumbling along the road when the foresters found them.

One second, the road was bleak and empty; the next it was full of rough looking men dressed in furs.

"What have we here?" One of the men asked.

"H h h help us," Paul stammered.

"Sure, we'll help you, but it needs to be a fair trade," the man walked around Paul and Daniel. "I've never seen a cloak like this before. We'd feed and warm you in exchange for the cloak."

Paul just nodded.

"OK then," the man said, "Help them along, quick now." The other men took Paul and Daniel's arms and half carried, half dragged them along a narrow track to where a large tent stood. The inside of the tent was so warm that Paul felt immediately sleepy. It reeked of stale food and drink and unwashed bodies. He thought it was heavenly.

"No going to sleep before you eat, or you might not wake up." A bowl was placed in Paul's hands. He ate the food and barely tasted it, but it was warm and filling. When the bowl was empty he closed his eyes and let sleep take him.

They spent the next day in the tent. The man who had traded for the sheepskin seemed to be the leader. All the men did what he said without hesitation.

"Where are your Books?" asked Paul when it was just the leader and him and Daniel in the tent.

"I have my Book in my tent," the man said, "and I am the Book for the rest of them. We'd never get any work done if they were always dashing off to check what the Book wanted them to do. When they sign on with me, their Books will just say to obey me."

"Ah," said Daniel, "I wondered how that would work." Paul looked at him and raised his eyebrows. "In our village everybody's job is different, so we each have our book that tells us how to do our job to not displease God. In a place where a lot of people do the same job, they wouldn't need different books as long as they knew who to follow."

"Smart guy," the other man said. "I've got to go check on the others. Stay here."

"Be careful," Daniel said when the man had left. "There is something going on here that I don't understand."

"At least we're warm."

"Yes," Daniel nodded his head. "But we don't have anything left to trade. So I don't know how we will get from here to where we are going without starving or freezing."

"Let me look at the Page," Paul said.

Two weeks.

"I wonder what that means," Paul said.

"If you had read 'twenty' before that woman offered you ten you wouldn't have known what that meant either."

"You think we're supposed to work for the foresters?"

"How else are we going to get to where we are going?"

"How else indeed?" the man said as he walked into the tent. "I can pay you one coin a day and you will be fed and kept warm while you work. You work for me until we reach Rym."

"Two weeks," Paul said.

"If we get delayed it might be longer than two weeks to get to the city. It doesn't take long to get cold and hungry.

"Two weeks," Paul said again.

"Very well then," the man said. "Give me your Book and let's get on with it."

Paul handed him the page reluctantly. The man looked at Daniel.

"That's the Book for both of us," Daniel said.

"Right then," the man held the Page up to them, "What does it say?"

OBEY

"Obey," they said together.

"Good, good." The man folded the Page and put it in his pocket. "You'll get this back in two weeks. Now that you work for me, you should know that my name is Liam, but you can call me Boss."

"Yes, Boss," Paul said.

"Yes, Boss," Daniel said.

"Well, enough lazing around. Let's get to work."

Paul found himself on his feet and following the Boss out of the tent. He didn't think about it. He couldn't have stopped himself if he'd tried.

Chapter 4

They wore furs that itched and stank but kept them warm. Paul and Daniel had the task of cutting the branches off the trees that the other men chopped down. It sounded safer than climbing high into the trees to cut off the top of the trees. Their job also meant that they could stand well out of the way when the great trees fell crashing to the ground. It was actually one of the most dangerous jobs that the foresters did. The last two men who trimmed branches were crushed when the tree shifted and rolled on top of them. It was their furs that Paul and Daniel wore.

Paul carried a large ax and crept up to the branch. He looked to check that Daniel was clear then swung the ax against the branch. Even though this branch was thicker than Paul's arm, it snapped like a twig and thumped onto the forest floor. The sharp scent of pine filled the air, but Paul didn't notice it any more, not anymore that he did the sore places where his hands stuck to the ax with sap. They had a potent smelling liquid that removed the sap at the end of the day. It was too precious to use more than that once. Paul envied the toppers who had tight fitting leather gloves to protect their skin. The Boss had just laughed when Paul inquired about them.

He moved to the next branch and repeated the swing. Daniel moved in closer and trimmed a branch that stuck out the other side. As long as they worked steadily, the Boss wouldn't tell them to hurry up. If they stopped for too long, he'd yell at them and they'd find themselves hacking at branches without regard for the danger. It was a balancing act between the danger and the need to keep the Boss happy.

Oddly, Paul enjoyed the work. He knew exactly what was expected of him, and he didn't need to struggle with alien concepts. There was a branch. He chopped the branch. There was another team behind them who would use a saw to cut the broken ends close to the trunk and trim the branches that stuck upwards into the air. That was almost as dangerous. The log could still roll and crush them. That's what had happened to the cook. He had hobbled around on his wooden leg for so long that he was quicker than most of the men with two good legs. Paul was getting stronger from swinging the axe and moving branches with the other crew. While Paul stepped back to let Daniel clear some branches on the other side, he daydreamed about Diana. He was careful to never lose focus, but thoughts of Diana kept him as warm as the furs he wore.

They reached the end of the log and looked for the next log. Daniel speculated endlessly about how the foresters would move the massive logs from the forest to the city.

The air was cold, but without the rain coming down it was dry and easy to keep warm. Snow fell and turned the forest white, but it didn't make them wet, so they didn't get cold. The harder Paul worked the warmer he felt. He only shivered in the morning between blanket and clothes when the chill air raised goosebumps on his skin.

Some shouting ahead signaled that something different had happened. A log had hung up in another tree next to it. The Boss was peering up at it. He wore the sheepskin cloak like it king's robes. He didn't look like a happy king. Paul walked over to join the other men looking up at the tangle.

"Paul, take a rope and run up the log. Tie yourself off to the standing tree, then start trimming the branches that are holding this beast up."

Paul snatched a rope from one of the men standing around watching and jumped up on the log. He wished that the Boss hadn't said *run up the log*. His legs didn't wait for him to plan a route but carried him in leaps and bounds up the sloped log to where the two trees tangled. Once he was there he stopped and assessed the situation.

It was a mess. If he hung over the outside of the log it could tear him loose and throw him to the ground when it broke free. If he went inside it could crush him between the falling log and standing tree. He thought that Boss had sent Daniel up to do this. Daniel was a lot smarter than he was. He needed to hurry or the

Boss would be yelling at him. What if he tied himself on the other side of the tree? That way if either he slipped, or the log slipped he had a chance of getting out of the way. He clambered through the thicket of branches to tie off to a large limb that was free of any of the fallen log's branches. That done, he climbed down underneath the log to see the fork in the tree that had caught and held the log.

He hoisted the ax off his back and made sure it was roped to his waist. Then he started chopping. He'd watched the other men doing ax work, and they took slow powerful strokes. Paul tried to match his swings to that. He was soon in a rhythm and cut a deep notch into the part of the trunk that held up the log.

The only warning he got was a sharp crack. Paul pushed away from his position and let the ax go. He held onto the rope that was tied around his waist and tried to control his swing. When he hit the tree on the far side he clung to the bark. The entire tree was shaking and creaking, then the log's weight pulled it away as half the tree's top fell to the ground.

The men were shouting, and at first Paul was afraid that the log or the top had landed on someone. Then he realized they were cheering. Shortly after the log fell, one of the top cutters climbed up beside him.

"The Boss told me to show you how to get down. Unless you feel like jumping."

Paul shook his head. The topper wrapped a flat braided rope around the tree and fastened both ends to Paul's belt. He scrambled up past Paul and undid the rope that fastened Paul to the tree then let it drop to the forest floor.

"Let yourself down against the slack like this," the topper said, showing Paul what he meant. "Then you lean into the tree and flick the rope down some. Not too far, mind." Again he showed Paul what to do. After a couple of tries Paul got the hang of it and lowered himself down out of the tree.

"Well done," the Boss said when Paul reached the ground. "Now, back to work." He slapped Paul on the shoulder and went off to supervise some other crew. Daniel and Paul walked to the stump end of the log and started trimming.

"The guys said that was a half and half job," Daniel said.

"What, that it worked half the time?"

"No, Paul, that the man died half the time."

Paul shuddered for a moment. He saw the way the trunk had fallen. It would have been easy to get caught by branches or log and crushed or thrown to the ground.

"You were using your head up there," Daniel said. "I think you had better than half a chance."

"I was trying to think like you up there," Paul said.

"It was clever. I saw the way you set up the rope to pull you away from trouble."

They worked through the rest of the day talking about the rope and how to do it next time. They both knew there would be a next time.

Paul sat in the tent and let his dinner settle. The men had the time after dinner to do as they pleased. Unless someone was getting out of control, the Boss gave no orders. Some of the men gambled with the money they hadn't been paid yet. They played a complex game with small bones. Daniel watched for a while and came away shaking his head.

"I don't know how they think they are going to win at that." He sat down beside Paul and sighed. "Maybe I'll just crawl off to bed."

"Soft southerners," one of the gamblers said. "I don't know how you expect to survive in the forest."

"We've managed so far."

"You've had it easy. The Boss should have left you on the road, or better yet, kept you for the cauldron-"

"Callam, be quiet," the Boss said from the corner of the tent where he sat carving a chunk of wood into some strange animal. Paul could see Callam fight to say something more, but finally he just turned and went back to the game. Paul followed Daniel out of the tent to the tiny tent they shared. Like their furs it had belonged to foresters who had died at their work.

The next day Paul had to free two logs that hung up in nearby trees. Both times he was able to swing to safety. The second log tore his fur as it passed. Paul could see that the Boss was getting angry. Each time the log hung up it was wasting time.

The third time a log hung up, he lost his temper.

"Callam," he yelled, "up and free that tree!"

"I'm a feller, not a squirrel," Callam shouted as he climbed up on the log.

"You're a squirrel if I say you're a squirrel!"

"Remember to tie the rope opposite where the log is hung up," Paul shouted to Callam.

"Watch how a real forester works, southerner." Callam ran up the tree and casually tossed his rope over the closest branch. He hung out over the log and swung the axe one handed. The branch snapped on the first swing. The log snagged him and pulled him from the tree. Callam's scream was cut short by the thump of the tree against the ground.

"A real forester is one who's alive," the Boss said. "Do it the Squirrel's way from now on. Go get Callam's gear," he said to Paul, "what you can stand to take. Then get back to work."

The other men took to calling Paul 'Squirrel' but he decided it was a mark of grudging respect.

One night while the others gambled the Boss sat down with Paul and Daniel.

"What brought you two here?" he asked.

"God sent me on a quest," Paul said. The Boss laughed, and the gamblers peered over briefly before they went back to the game.

"You're serious, aren't you?" The Boss shook his head. "I'm happy that God doesn't see fit to meddle in my affairs. I do my work by the Book and count myself lucky.

"Why were you on that road in the rain?" Daniel asked.

"Needed to scout out a path to draw the logs to the road. The drayers won't haul the logs from where they fall, will they?"

"Drayers?"

"Men who run the big wagons to haul the logs to Rym. Don't work for them if you think I'm tough." The Boss pushed himself to his feet. "Don't be trusting God to be doing all your thinking for you. the Book will tell you how to do something, but you still need to learn the lessons. There are a lot of ways to die following the Book." He went and watched over the gamers' shoulders for a while before sitting in his usual place in the corner.

No more logs got hung up before the Boss announced one morning that they were to pack up. It was time to meet up with the drayers and take the logs to the city.

They struck camp and packed all their gear into packs like Paul's. Paul gave Daniel Callam's pack and they stuffed the tent and extra furs into it. He also had a long knife that was nearly the length of Paul's forearm. He had no idea what he would use it for, but perhaps he could trade it in Rym.

Soon they were at the road and the drayers arrived. They led huge horses that were chained to the sections of log. They pulled the logs to the road where other men used a complicated system of ropes and levers to load the logs onto wagons.

It was a day's work to make sure all the logs were ready for the drayers. Then the foresters got ready to make their way into the woods to cut more logs.

"You won't consider staying on?" the Boss asked. "You're both good workers."

"No," Paul said. "We have to get on to Rym."

"If you need work again, ask for Liam. I'll treat you fair." the Boss handed the Page back to Paul, then he counted out fourteen coins. "Keep the gear as a bonus." He was turning away then came back to Paul. "You were wise to hold to a limited term. It might be months before I need to get to the city. Remember that. the Book around here isn't as forgiving as you're used to."

Paul went up to the head drayer.

"I need work to get us to Rym."

"What do I need with a pair of greenhorns?" the drayer said. "The city's that way." He pointed north. "Two days if you walk smartly and don't get caught in the snow."

"We've already had snow," Paul said.

"This ain't snow," the other man said. "You don't want to get caught out in a real snow fall."

"We'd better get going then," Daniel said. They hoisted their packs to their backs and started away up the road. Soon the sound of shouting faded and it was just them and the crunch of their boots in the snow.

<u>Chapter 5</u>

The world went from dim to bright in seconds as they stepped out of the gloom beneath the trees. Paul's eyes leaked water as he squinted ahead. White light from sun on the snowy fields knifed into his head. Eventually his eyes adjusted and he could look properly. Rym was beyond anything Paul had imagined. It was a huge anthill of activity. He could see people lined up at the gates. Even from this far away he could smell the city.

Paul and Daniel joined a thickening crowd of people walking or riding toward the city. He watched a rider kick someone with a sack out of the way of his horse. Paul made sure to give the people with horses plenty of space. The man with sack didn't complain, he just picked himself and his sack up and joined the flow again.

"Foresters?" one of the guards said when they'd reached the gates. "You got work in the city?"

"We worked with the foresters;" Daniel said. "We'll find work in Rym."

"Ain't much to do in the winter," the guard said. "We have our own way of dealing with folks who can't pay their own way."

"We'll keep that in mind," Paul said.

"Fine then, see that you do." The guard handed them a little dark green ribbon. "You wear this and obey anybody but those wearing grey."

"So it's like working for the foresters," Paul said.

"It's nothing like working for the foresters," the guard said. "They might care if you live or die. Get in the wrong person's way here and you'll end up in the Cauldron. Now put on the ribbons or go away."

"These are only for in the city?" asked Daniel.

"Do you want them or not?" The guard looked like he was going to put them away.

"We'll take them," Paul said. They pinned the ribbons onto their furs. The guard pointed to the blue ribbon on his uniform.

"Go," he said, "and stay out of trouble."

Paul and Daniel walked into the city and were immediately lost in the maze of streets. The vast majority of people wore either grey or green ribbons. They made sure to give wide berth to anyone with a different coloured ribbon.

"Now what?" Daniel asked.

"I'll check the Page," Paul said.

Turn around

"What?" Paul asked, but Daniel turned around. A big man was pushing a cart filled with vegetables, but he was struggling to get it moving through the crowds. He wore a grey ribbon and nobody seemed too concerned about getting out of his way.

"May we help you?" Paul asked.

"What?" The man looked up. "Oh, foresters. I can't hire you." He tapped the grey ribbon.

"We're new to the city," Paul said. "We'd be happy to help in exchange for some guidance."

"Oh, very well." The man put the shafts of the cart down. "You push the cart and I'll make a path. We may make it to the market before it closes, after all."

With both Paul and Daniel pushing, the cart was easy to move. The man cleared a path by the simple expedient of walking through the crowds and forcing everyone else to move out of his way. They arrived in a square that was even more thickly packed with people than the streets. Now, what slowed them down were people trying to buy the vegetables from the owner of the cart. The market was louder than anything Paul had ever heard. If he weren't pushing on the cart he'd have put his hand over his ears. The man ahead of them didn't slow for the noise, nor did he step aside from the reeking lumps on the road Paul learned to avoid since they made him slip. If this was a great city, he was glad to live in a tiny village. A desire to drop the cart and flee back to Eben struck him like a blow. He fought tears back from his eyes. He needed to be able to see, but for the next few steps he only saw blurred movements that struck him as being as harsh as noise or odour.

Finally, they arrived at an empty space just big enough for the cart.

"Late again?" The man standing in the space beside them had a cart that was covered with old clothes.

"Harald's gone to the cauldron," the big man said.

"So, you're working with foresters now?"

"They were handy."

"Huh." The other man turned to try to sell his wares to a woman wearing a grey ribbon.

"People don't like foresters?" Paul said.

"Foresters are used to the freedoms of the woods," the man said. "They don't do well in the city."

"So what do we need to know?"

"Where do I start?" the big man said. He interrupted himself to sell a cabbage to a woman. "You're used to having one Boss. Most of the time the Boss is reasonable cause you don't make money long by abusing your crew. You come here, you forget to watch the ribbons. Sure enough you get in the road of a blue or even, the Book forbid, a Red and the next thing you know you're off to the Cauldron."

"What's this Cauldron that people keep talking about?"

"It's bad luck to talk about it."

"OK," Daniel said, "so aside from that, what do we need to watch for?"

"You'll want to get hired on." The man sold a bag of potatoes. "Or the guards will be after you. Nobody will hire you, looking like foresters."

Daniel nudged Paul and pointed to the next cart.

"Maybe we should be trading in our furs."

"What do I want with forester furs," the man said when they asked him. "Who's going to buy them?"

"Foresters?" Paul said.

The man snorted but dug into the pile. "I might be able to let these go."

Paul wanted to look at the Page for advice, but it would mean digging through all his furs. Nobody else was carrying a Book, or a Page. He didn't want to stand out even more.

"We need clothes for both of us," Paul said, "Ones without holes in them."

It took a while, but when they were done Paul and Daniel were dressed in woolen clothes that were a couple of steps up from being rags. The clothes seller stroked the furs in a way that suggested strongly he got the better part of the deal.

"You stay and gloat," the vegetable man said. "Watch my wagon and I'll take these fellows over to the labour market. The clothes seller grunted but was selling onions to a passerby before they got out of earshot.

The labour market was a large square full of both men and women who wandered about looking at posters describing work that needed to be done. Sometimes one of them would stop and talk to a person beside the poster whose ribbon had a red stripe. Most of the time the person would shake their head at the hopeful job seeker.

Paul saw that there were a great many more people than there were posters.

"Good luck," the vegetable man said and left them there. Paul headed toward one of the posters.

"What does a footman do?" he wondered out loud.

"If you don't know, you can't do the job," said the woman who stood beside the poster. She made a shooing motion with her hands and Paul moved on. Most of the posters were the same, calling for work that he couldn't even define, never mind do.

He stopped in front of a poster. Grounds keeper.

"I used to be a farmer," Paul said.

"You know anything about gardens?" the man beside the poster asked.

"I grew vegetables for the village, kept a ewe sheep too."

"Know anything about roses?"

"No, I only grew vegetables."

"Good," the man said, "You might do. Do you know anything about peafowl?"

"My friend raised chickens."

"Then you had better go find him," the man said. "If the job is still open, when you get back, we'll talk."

Paul stood and looked around the crowed square. Where would Daniel be? He wasn't behind Paul. None of those jobs would be good for Daniel either, so he must have gone the other way. He jogged through the crowd until he saw Daniel. People jostled and muttered at him, but Paul didn't care. *I'm already becoming one of them*, he thought.

"Hurry," he said, "I may have found us some work." Daniel followed him back to where the man was shaking his head at a young woman. She looked to be at the point of tears. She walked away and vanished into the crowd.

"Ah," the man said, "we will proceed to the Master's estate and I will determine if you are able to do the work we need." They followed him out of the square and through the streets. The streets became progressively less crowded, but the people who were there wore red ribbons or at least had a red stripe on their grey. No one paid the slightest attention to them. They arrived at a gate in a wall that was at least eight feet tall. The man opened the gate and let them through. He closed the gate behind them.

They entered a garden that was the size of their village back home. It wasn't much to look at in the winter, but Paul was sure in the warm months that it was a riot of colour. The man led them along a path, then ducked through a gap in a hedge that paralleled the path. Paul nodded as soon as he saw the garden. This was his kind of garden. He wandered up and down the side of the garden murmuring approval as he went. His homesickness came back, but he pushed it away. He was on a quest.

"If you have a garden like this, you hardly need me," Paul said to the man who'd brought him here.

"If the boy can recognize that, I can use him." An older man came out of a shed. He was leaning on a stick. It was obvious he was in pain as he moved.

"He knows nothing of roses."

"So much the better."

"Come," the first man said to Daniel, "let us see if you are as fortunate as your friend."

"You can call me Gardener. You are Grounds Keeper, or you will be if you work out."

"My name is Paul."

"Yes, yes, I'm sure," Gardener said. "But the Master and his family aren't to be bothered with names. Get used to answering to Grounds Keeper or go back to the market."

"Then I will learn to like Grounds Keeper."

"Wise of you."

"Now show me my garden." Gardener waved his stick over the garden and Paul looked over the expanse.

"Well," he said, "it looks like you have winter carrots here and parsnips..."

Later that night he and Daniel compared notes. They both wore ribbons with red strips on the grey. They also had small badges that marked them as working at this particular estate.

"I'm not sure the stables will be any warmer than our tent," Paul said, "but I don't think they'll be any colder either."

"I'll be glad to sleep on something other than the ground, even if it is hay," Daniel said.

"So we are both to be called Grounds Keeper," Paul said. "It seems strange to both have the same name."

"Not name, but label," Daniel said. "It is too much work for the Master to learn who the people are who keep his home, so we are called by the work that we do."

"It seems the world gets stranger the further we get from home."

"It makes sense if you think on it," Daniel said. "There are too many people here to simply do as their Book tells them. It is more efficient to have some people who have Books, while others simply obey the ones with the Books. It is like the foresters, but even more so. The ribbons are different. They separate us into the obedient and the must be obeyed. There is a compulsion so the ones to be obeyed don't have to waste time explaining things.

"Yet it seems hard on those who must simply obey."

"I don't recall anywhere in the Book where it says that the world should be fair," Daniel said. "We obey or we displease God. If we are to start questioning, who's to say where it would end?"

Chapter 6

Life on the estate is easier than in the forest. Paul thought as he worked in the garden. *We don't need to worry about trees falling on us or branches snapping and taking our heads off.*

Paul dug the potatoes that the kitchen would cook at supper. A young woman he hadn't seen before wandered into the garden. She wore a pure red ribbon and a large house badge in gold thread on her breast.

"Grounds Keeper," she said, "come here."

Paul put his fork into the earth and walked over to the young woman.

"My boot is untied."

Paul stood there for a moment before he realized she meant for him to tie it. He knelt down and retied the laces. His hands were awkward in the bitter air.

"What a terribly ugly bow," the young woman said. She pushed Paul over with her foot. "Remain there until the Gardener comes. Tell him I said to beat you."

Paul lay helpless in the dirt for the remainder of the afternoon. He tried to get up, but his muscles refused to obey him. The cold seeped into his body and soul. He would never have imagined being so helpless before he set out on this journey. He didn't like the feeling but it was becoming all too familiar to him. The cook came out.

"Grounds Keeper," she said into the garden, "I need some carrots." Then she turned her head and saw Paul and sighed and left again. In a little while the Gardener came.

"Get up, Grounds Keeper," he said, "I suppose she wants you beaten."

"Yes, Gardener."

The old man rapped Paul on the shins with his stick.

"That should do." He turned to go back into the house. "Finish the potatoes, the Book knows we can't let things like this get in the way of our work."

Paul told Daniel about the incident while they prepared to sleep that night.

"It seems strange that her Book tells her to abuse her staff so," Paul said.

"It may not state her responsibilities in quite that manner," Daniel said. "I expect her Book says something along the lines of keeping the staff in order and this is just the way that she finds to do it. The Book gives more latitude here than at home."

"Why would that be?" Paul said, "Are these people not just as much at risk of displeasing God as the people in our village?"

"It is a mystery, Paul," Daniel said. "But I've never claimed to understand the Book. It is about obedience, not understanding."

"I suppose so." Paul wasn't happy with the answer, but he couldn't imagine an alternative. He closed his eyes and went to sleep. He felt his legs twitching in the night as if they still shook off their enforced immobility.

The heavy snows came. Just walking through the snow was difficult. It melted and soaked into clothing and boots. Paul filled his time shoveling the path so that the masters of the estate didn't need to struggle through the inconvenience. Every once in a while, the young woman would seek him out and demand that he tie her boot. Though he practiced carefully, he could never tie a knot that pleased her. Paul often spent long times in the snow waiting for the Gardener to be fetched, so he could have a rap on the shins and be freed to go back to work. *What am I doing in this place?* The days were endlessly repetitive, yet Paul woke with a feeling that he inhabited a strange world that he'd never seen before. He stopped looking at the Page. It did nothing but counsel patience.

One day Gardener came and fetched Paul.

"You've not worked with the cauldron spawn have you?"

"No, Gardener," Paul said.

"Come," the old man said and headed off with his stick. Paul followed. They came to the wide open space in front of the house where the Master's peers parked their carriages. A group of men dressed in rags were listlessly shoveling snow into a wagon.

"Just watch them and keep them on task," Gardener said. "You're their Book, you must tell them each step to do. See?" He pointed to one man who was shoveling an already cleared spot. He moved the man until he was again shoveling snow. The men had an odd smell like meat that had just started to turn. It unsettled Paul. He tried to breathe through his mouth, but the odour pervaded everything.

"What happened to them?"

"They are the cauldron spawn." Gardener said, "Their will has been taken from them lest they displease God and doom us all."

"We don't have anything like this at home," Paul said.

"No, you wouldn't would you?" Gardener said and he walked away.

Paul spent the remainder of the day prodding and guiding the cauldron spawn. His awareness of their odour faded as his frustration grew. They didn't understand instructions other than 'start' or 'stop'. He had to physically move them into position, then watch them carefully to make sure that they didn't wander into trouble. If all people were as stupid as the cauldron spawn it would be impossible not to displease God. Paul felt a shiver down his spine at the thought. What if God were as frustrated with him as he was with the cauldron born?

That evening he pulled out the Page for the first time in weeks.

Find the Cauldron

Paul stared at the page for a long time, but the words didn't change. Daniel came in and went over to his bed.

"Have you seen the Cauldron spawn?" Paul asked.

"Yes," Daniel said, "they are dead."

"I know they are stupid," Paul said, "but dead?"

"We burn wood to warm the greenhouse where the peacocks roam. The cauldron spawn chop the wood. I saw one cut off his own hand and throw it in the fire. Then it tried to pick up the ax like it still had two hands. There was no blood, no cry of pain."

"Why would the Book allow such a thing?"

"How could a dead man displease God?" Daniel said. "If it weren't for how stupid they were, I think we would all be cauldron spawn. As it is they are only good for the most basic of tasks."

He rolled over and went to sleep.

Daniel's work must be even more taxing than Paul's. He had taken to coming in and going immediately to sleep. This was more conversation than they had had in a week. Paul hadn't even had a chance to tell him that they were to find the Cauldron.

Something woke Paul up in the middle of the night. He rolled over to see Daniel slipping in under his blankets. Something in Daniel's face stopped Paul from saying anything.

For the next few nights, Paul laid awake while Daniel slipped out of the stable and went somewhere. Daniel didn't have a Book or the Page to tell him what to do. Someone must have told him to go in the middle of the night. Paul had a vision of the young woman, the Master's daughter sneering at him while he lay helpless in the snow.

Feeling sick to his stomach, he turned to the Page.

Wait. Follow.

The next night, Daniel slept through the night and the night after that. Paul was beginning to think that he had imagined everything. But then Daniel slipped out in the night and Paul crawled out of his blankets. He stuffed the Page in his shirt and followed after.

He immediately wished that he had put on a cloak or something, but it was too late now. Daniel walked through the icy night as if it were summer. He came to a door in the house and slipped through it. Paul followed, and the heat was welcome, but he didn't dare lose track of Daniel. Neither did he want to be seen. He was certain that they would not be welcome in this house. Daniel walked quietly but confidently through the halls to a door. A woman inside with a grey badge and a red stripe was waiting for him. For a moment Paul thought it was her Daniel was meeting, then she pushed the door open and the young woman was standing there, nude, waiting for him. The look on her face wasn't one of delight, but of cruelty.

She pulled Daniel into the room and Paul caught a glimpse of his face. It looked one of the Cauldron spawn, like he had lost all ability to think for himself. Paul must have made a slight noise because the woman who waited outside the room made frantic shooing motions at him.

Too late, Paul realized there was someone behind him.

"What are you doing here?" The voice compelled an answer from Paul. He turned to see the red ribbon and gold house badge of the Master, as he heard his voice say that he was following his friend who was even now in the Master's daughter's room.

By following Daniel he had doomed them both.

"So, you are waiting your turn to defile my daughter?"

"No, Master," Paul's voice said, "she doesn't like me."

The Master's face went hard and bleak.

"You will stay silent, unless I speak to you. When questioned you will say that you have subverted the Book. You are a Chooser and you wish to displease God."

Paul tried to open his mouth to argue, but he couldn't speak. The Master turned away and walked to the door and banged on the door after telling the servant woman to stay.

He hadn't told Paul to stay. Paul retraced his steps through the house, ducking into alcoves to avoid the people who ran toward the noise at the other end of the house. Once outside of the house he ran to the stables and packed their gear. There might be a way to rescue Daniel, but only if he stayed free himself.

Paul loaded the pack on his shoulders and walked to the door. He would escape, then the Page would help him rescue Daniel. He opened the door, and the Master stood there with a cruel smile on his face.

"I knew you would try to flee," he said. "You all do. Dump out your pack." Paul felt his hands turning the pack over and watched as all his and Daniel's gear poured out on the threshold.

It looked like rags in the snow. The big knife that they had taken from Callam's gear thudded out last. The Master picked it up and looked at it.

"This weapon alone can send you to the Cauldron," he said, "even if you weren't already going there." He pulled the knife from the sheath. "Cheap steel, it won't hold its edge past one use." He stabbed Paul in the stomach with the knife. When he pulled the knife out he pulled it across the back of his hand. It made a faint cut. "See," he said, "dull already." He stabbed Paul again. This time he left the knife in the wound. When the servants came they stared in shock as Paul fell to the floor. Paul gasped through the pain of the knife in his stomach. He tried to make his hands grip the knife to pull it out, but they refused to obey. It was like after the daughter left him helpless in the snow, but now instead of the cold seeping in, Paul's life blood leaked out. He watched from the floor, unable to speak, barely able to breathe without feeling the stab of the blade again.

"Look," the Master said and held up his hand. "He tried to stab me. the Book says I must protect my family." The people nodded. "Take him and the other ones to the Cauldron." Paul lay on the floor and wondered who else besides him and Daniel were going to the Cauldron.

The servants lifted him up and dumped him roughly on a wagon. Daniel and the woman from the hallway were already there. Daniel looked almost relieved, but the woman glared at Paul as if she could stab him again with her eyes. The wagon bounced through the streets and Paul moaned with each bump. He wondered why he wasn't dead yet. Maybe he would die before they got to the Cauldron. The pain was still there, but it started to move away from him as if he didn't occupy his own body and it was someone else's stomach that bled around the steel blade.

For some reason Paul started remembering Diana. She would be so disappointed when he never came home. She had wasted her kiss, but he held on to the memory of her lips and the taste of honey and the soft feel of her body against his. The memories pushed the pain further away. He felt cold in his stomach now. Like he'd been lying in the snow all day.

The wagon pulled into a courtyard and men in black uniforms came out and directed Cauldron spawn to drag them from the wagon. The spawn awkwardly took hands and feet of the three people and carried them into the building.

They were carried along a dank corridor until they reached a platform that hung out over a huge cauldron. It was bigger than Paul had imagined possible. *I found it,* he thought to God. *Much good that's going to do.*

<u>Chapter 7</u>

A man in the same black uniform as the rest, but with a gold ribbon on his breast, walked out and nudged each one of them with his toe. He grimaced in disgust when he saw that he had Paul's blood on his boot.

"Lord Galway always did have a temper," the man said. "Yet he has done you a favour. Soon you will be unable to conceive of anything that would displease God." Paul wanted to say something, though he wasn't sure of the shape of the words, but he couldn't force the words out past the blood in his mouth. "Don't you think it's marvelous?"

"This pleases God?" Daniel said.

"The Book requires me to keep order in my domain. What better way to keep order than to remove the desire for disorder?" The man walked to the railing and looked out over the Cauldron. "Can you believe that when God gave this to my ancestor it could be held in one hand? Each person who goes into the cauldron makes it slightly bigger. My counselors believe it is the will of the people that they leave in the cauldron that feeds it." He looked lovingly over the vast cauldron. "It is that will that we tap to make the ribbons and the badges so that everyone knows their place." He came and crouched down over Daniel, "Or at least most people. There are always those who must be given to the Cauldron because they refuse their place in the world."

"This is still wrong," Daniel said.

"How can it be wrong? It is written in the Book of my Kingdom. I would show it to you, but then I would have to kill you. The cauldron spawn are so much more useful when they go in alive. "

Paul felt a flutter inside his shirt. The Page was trying to tell him something. He pawed at his shirt, but he couldn't get his hands to work properly. The man with the gold ribbon pulled out the Page from Paul's shirt.

"How quaint," he said,"a page from a Book. He held up the page so Paul and Daniel could see it. "What am I?" he said to them,

King

Paul stared in despair at the page. This madness was in the Book. Then the words shifted.

Drink the Cauldron

Neither the King nor Daniel seemed to notice the new words. The King went on speaking as if the Page were showing exactly what he expected it too. He started trying to drag himself to the edge of the platform.

"Let me show you," he said, "Get up Maid, and jump into the Cauldron."

The woman climbed to her feet. With a look of absolute terror she walked to the edge of the platform and leaped. She let out a terrible shriek as she fell into the liquid, but as soon as her head went under the liquid it stopped. A moment later a grey hand clasped the edge of the Cauldron and a cauldron spawn pulled itself out. It fell to the floor and twitched a few times before a man in a black uniform stepped out of the shadows and guided the spawn away.

Paul reached the edge and looked down. He was dead anyway so he pushed himself over the edge and fell toward the seething liquid. Only he landed on the rim, half in, half out of the Cauldron. The agony from the knife made him scream. Liquid from the cauldron filled his mouth and he swallowed. Greasy and vile, it tasted like the smell of the cauldron spawn. If he'd been able, Paul would have vomited it up.

Drinking the fluid was like being stabbed by the knife again and again. Each moment grew more painful. Paul wanted to scream, or cry, but he couldn't. His body was no longer under his control. Paul's mouth stretched wide open and he swallowed the liquid without stopping.

Impossibly, the Cauldron started shrinking. Paul heard the King shouting for him to stop, but he could no more stop than he could have stopped falling if he fell from a tree. The pain continued unabated and Paul's vision changed. It was as if he had always seen the world as a painting flat on a wall and suddenly it gained depth and movement. He was taking in more than pain. He drank in despair and defeat. He swallowed cruelty and lies. Paul wondered how the Book could allow such darkness in the world, but then he saw something that turned him red with rage. the Books were a lie. Some Books were filled with honesty and hope, others with sick desires that were sated in pain and blood. The King was right. This Cauldron was in his Book. Paul could see it as if it were his own Book open on the counter in his kitchen.

The Books didn't come from God, or at least not the God that came to him in his home. He didn't know where they came from, but he knew they weren't from God. The idea that all his life had been given to a lie overwhelmed the rage with grief. It wasn't just him. It was Daniel and Diana too who were living the lie.

Paul was standing on the floor now and he put his arms around the huge pot and lifted. He drank in grief over all the people who were deceived. He loved them and wanted to free them. The greatest pain of all struck him then. He couldn't free them. It wasn't in his power to. Even God could not, or would not strike the blindness from their eyes. All his people were trapped by their desire to not fail God. By not failing God, they were failing themselves.

The pot had become a cup now. Where it had been huge and black, now it was crystal and the liquid shone white between his fingers. The cup shrank to a thimble and then it vanished.

Paul looked down at himself and saw that the knife still stuck in him. He pulled it out and let it drop to the floor where it shattered like glass. Guards in black surrounded him and pointed swords at him. The King was shouting incoherently at them. One of them shrugged and stabbed Paul with his sword. Paul felt a burning pain as the steel sliced through him, but as the guard withdrew the sword the wound vanished. Another guard tried with the same result. He felt a power in him that he didn't understand. The cauldron had irrevocably changed him. He knew that in his bones. The power moved like blood through him. It gave him words.

"You, King," Paul said, "come down here." He held up his hand between him and the guards. "Enough." The guards stepped back until their backs were against the wall. One by one their swords shattered. "Go," Paul said, "go home. Find your own way." He knew with great sadness that they would find a Book waiting for them, as each person living in Rym old enough to read would find a Book waiting for them. They weren't free. It was just a different set of chains.

The King had reached the floor and held a knife to Daniel's throat.

"I want my Cauldron back," the King said.

Paul knew he could do it. Somehow he could pull all that force and will out of himself and shape it into another Cauldron.

"No," he said, and flicked a finger at the King's knife. It flung across the room and stuck into the stone wall. The King let go of Daniel and stepped back.

"Who sent you?" he demanded, "What enemy sent you to destroy my Kingdom?"

"Your Kingdom stands," Paul said, "You will just need to find a different way to rule it."

"My Book," the King said, "I must read my Book." He fled from the room and Paul put him out of his mind. The King would only find different lies in his Book, but there was nothing he could do about that.

"Are you OK?" Paul asked Daniel. Daniel tried to speak, then collapsed in tears at Paul's feet. Paul put his hand on Daniel's shoulder and let him weep. There would be time enough to talk as they took on the next part of the quest. He put out his hand and the Page floated through the air to land on his hand. It was covered with blood, but Paul could still read the words.

West. Find the Sword.

<u>Chapter 8</u>

Paul guided Daniel out of the room that once held the Cauldron. They passed the body of the woman from the hallway. All the cauldron spawn were truly dead now. He wasn't sure how long his apparent invulnerability would last. He didn't really want to experiment in case it suddenly vanished; even the swords didn't kill him, they still hurt.

They made it to the courtyard. Bodies of the cauldron spawn lay everywhere. Guards shouted at each other. Paul walked Daniel through the middle of it as if they were alone. Out in the city, there was less chaos. People hadn't yet discovered that the ribbons were no longer effective. Paul thought that they would probably continue to obey out of habit.

They stumbled along the street. They had no gear, no food, and Daniel was still shaking with great heaving sobs. Snow fell from the heavens as if it wanted to smother Rym completely.

"You don't want to go out there tonight," the guard at the gate said. "It's sure death in this weather."

"Death is everywhere," Paul said. The guard shrugged and let him pass.

They walked along the road until Daniel couldn't walk any more. The snow coated them and moisture ran down Paul's back. The chill was real, but like the swords it didn't affect him. He brushed the snow from Daniel's shoulders and walked until Daniel could no longer move. Paul used a stick to dig out a shelter at the edge of the road and they crawled in. To Paul's surprise it was warmer under the snow than outside. He held Daniel close and went to sleep.

He woke in the morning when Daniel pushed away from him and crawled outside. Paul followed him.

"I don't know what you are anymore," Daniel said. "What you did was impossible."

"I'm not so sure myself," Paul said. "God isn't done with me yet."

"I'm done with God," Daniel said.

"Journey with me away from here," Paul said. "Then you can return home while I travel west."

"What's west?"

"A Sword."

"I would think the last thing you would want to find is a sword." Daniel ran a finger along one of the scars that peeked out through the tears in Paul's shirt. "I'm surprised that the guards didn't try to stop you as a cauldron spawn."

"The snow was heavy. I don't think they could see very well."

"So what happened to you?"

"I drank in all the life that was in the Cauldron. The King thought it was the will of the people he threw in there that made it grow, but it was their life. All the pain and sorrow and fear, but love and joy too. It's hard to describe."

"I'll bet." Daniel was silent for a long time. "We might as well be walking. I, at least, feel the cold."

"I feel it too," Paul said. "I still experience pain and cold and hunger. It just has no affect on me physically."

"Must be nice."

"I'm not sure," Paul said. "I don't know what Diana would think."

"I think she'd be glad to have you home however you came."

"Maybe."

Paul walked ahead and pushed a trail through the deep snow for Daniel. Each night he dug out a shelter in the snow and they would huddle in its warmth.

"She came to me in the greenhouse," Daniel said one night as they huddled in a dark snow cave. Paul didn't need to ask who. "She admired me and I was flattered. She's beautiful, at least on the outside. One day she commanded me to kiss her. I couldn't not obey her command. She bit my lip and tasted my blood. She commanded me not to speak of it. Each day she came back and claimed a bit more of my soul. Until she commanded me to attend her in her room. Even while I was trembling in fear, I was trembling with desire too. I wanted her. "

"When you followed me, I knew it was over. But I couldn't refuse her. I hoped that I would die quickly and be free. At the same time, I hoped to live forever trapped in her web."

"You were compelled."

"Yes. No. I don't know." Daniel sighed. "I might have succumbed even without the ribbon. She was beautiful, and I was just a chicken farmer pretending to be a Grounds Keeper. Perhaps if I'd kept my Book, I would have been OK."

"The Books aren't what we always thought them to be," Paul said.

"What do you mean?"

"I don't think God would force us to eat oatmeal three times a week if she didn't like it herself."

"So where did the Books come from?"

"God wasn't alone in the Garden with the man and the woman."

Daniel didn't say anything else, but the next day he climbed out of their snow cave and stretched until his bones popped.

"Let's go," Daniel said. "We'll find the foresters and get some food."

"We'll have to work for it."

"A couple of weeks would be worth it to be warm and fed again."

Later that day they saw a track running off from the road. They found Liam and the foresters cutting smaller trees and stacking the logs.

"You want to work again?" Liam asked.

"Two weeks," Daniel said.

"Two weeks then," Liam said. "Same rate. What happened to all the gear you had?"

"You don't want to know."

"Right, you had to sell it to live in the city. Probably didn't get half what it was worth either." Liam handed them each an ax. "Things have changed. I don't want to be the guy who orders everyone around. So either you work or you don't get fed. You cause trouble and you're out on your ear. Make sure you explain it to your friend there."

"That's Paul, um Squirrel," Daniel said.

"You're kidding." Liam peered at Paul for a long moment. "I guess so, but you sure look different. The eyes I think. I don't think Callam would have messed with you the way you look now."

"I work just the same," Paul said.

"You'd better!" Liam said and gave them a shove. "Go, get swinging those axes."

They were cutting firewood now. The drayers came up each week and hauled away a pile of logs on long runners. Paul and Daniel still were trimming branches. One branch caught Paul across the face and knocked him to the ground. Liam came running over as Paul pushed himself to his hands and knees.

"I thought you were dead," he said. "Be more careful."

Paul just nodded, still crouched down and facing the ground. He waited until Liam's back was turned and pulled a long sliver of wood from his eye.

"Doesn't that hurt?" Daniel asked.

"Yes," Paul said, "but probably less than leaving it there."

They worked for the two weeks, then Liam paid them their penny a day. He let them buy the furs they were wearing and some food for the rest of their journey South. They travelled mostly in silence. The snow was deep enough that they could clamber over the massive tree across the road. When the temperature plummeted one night, Paul gave Daniel his furs.

"I'm more comfortable with them," he said, "but I don't need them. You do." Paul sat through the nights feeling the cold, but it not touching him. He didn't need to sleep either. Paul didn't think he was quite human anymore. He thought he should find some sorrow in that thought, but he couldn't reach it. He put his hands up to his face. Liam hadn't recognized him. What if Diana didn't recognize him? He wasn't dreaming about the kiss any more. Now, he thought about the smile she gave him and how she looked walking ahead of him to the cheese room. The feelings were a just a pale shade of the warmth he remembered feeling, but he still smiled in the darkness.

Daniel made him put the furs back on before they reached the village with the market.

"They are going to be asking enough questions without you walking in like it's a summer day."

Paul didn't argue, but put the furs on. They walked into Cepha and stopped in the market long enough to buy some bread and dry cheese. Nobody remembered them from the last time so they turned and walked west toward the river.

"It's only a couple of days from home," Paul said as they left town. "By the time you get down the mountain the snow will be gone and you can be home."

"And have Diana asking me why I left you alone?" Daniel said. "I don't think so. God made me your companion, so you're stuck with me until we're done."

"OK then," Paul said. "Let's go."

The road was packed and well used. Paul and Daniel saw a number of people on the road going in either direction. Nobody seemed to be in a hurry. Several times they stopped to share a meal with fellow travelers. They ate whatever their hosts prepared without comment, but on their own they stuck with the bread and cheese they'd bought.

"I don't want to eat another bowl of oatmeal for the rest of my life." Daniel said.

Paul just shrugged. "It's all food."

"It's sad," Daniel said, "the pain doesn't touch you, but neither does anything else."

"I guess that's true," Paul said. "It's getting hard to tell."

Daniel just shook his head.

They arrived at the river and found a bustling town that focused on moving goods either off the river and east, or from the east onto boats that took the goods south. The people in Cepha had told them it was called Brurn.

Paul and Daniel headed down to the docks to find some way of getting on a boat going south.

Paul noticed immediately that the people walked very differently. Some like him walked upright and straight. Others walked with a rolling gait that made them look like the ground they walked on was perpetually moving. They discovered that these were the sailors.

They soon learned that the sailors weren't interested in taking on novice sailors to go south.

"I don't know," Daniel said. "We don't have enough to pay for the trip, and no one wants to hire us."

Paul pulled out the Page. He hadn't looked at it since he read Sword through his own blood.

Slave

"That's certainly helpful," Daniel said. "We don't want to be slaves. That's what we escaped in the north."

"True enough," Paul said. "But we might not have much choice unless we want to starve here. We're out of both food and coin again."

"I'm not becoming a slave," Daniel said, "and neither are you."

"Slave market's at the South Dock," a passing sailor said. "Buying or selling, that's where you have to go."

They walked down to the southernmost point of the town. The river foamed under the docks and roared away south. They watched a boat spin and bob on the current. Paul was sure it was going to be torn apart when it suddenly righted itself and sped off out of sight.

"The first bit is the tricky part, gentlemen."

Paul looked to see a middle aged sailor standing next to them.

"We need to get on a boat," Daniel said.

"The only ones who ride on my boat are slaves," the sailor said.

"Your boat?" asked Daniel.

"I'm the Captain."

"I'll go as a slave," Paul said. "My friend rides as a free man."

"No!" Daniel said, "You can't do that."

"It's OK, Daniel," Paul said. "I'm sure it will work out."

"No..."

"It's either this or you go home."

"You come home with me."

"I can't, remember? I have no home to go to."

Daniel stared at Paul for a long time, then he sighed. "OK, have it your way."

"I haven't agreed to this insanity," the captain said.

"You will," Paul said. "Lead us to your boat."

"If you're going to be a slave, you'll have to get rid of that attitude."

They reached the boat to learn that his cook had fallen and broken a leg. He gave Paul a strange look.

"I should just forget you."

"There are other captains, other boats," Paul said.

"But what will happen to me and mine if I refuse you?"

Paul shrugged.

"You can cook, right?" the captain asked Daniel.

"I won't poison you, if that's what you're asking," he said.

"He can cook well enough," Paul said.

"Well, I need to draw blood," the captain said.

Paul put out his arm.

"By the Book, you have a lot of scars."

"One more won't matter then."

"It ain't the scar that matters," the captain said. "It's the blood. It will bind you body and soul to whoever buys you."

"Body," Paul said, "not soul. I'm not sure that's mine."

"Well I don't care, as long as I get my money." He drew a line down Paul's forearm and collected the blood in a tiny bottle. "Whoever owns this, owns you. You ain't the first one to sell themselves thinking to be free on the other end, even if you're one of the strangest."

Chapter 9

The hold of the boat was close and hot in spite of the cold outside. The slaves weren't chained; the door to the hold wasn't even locked, but they were trapped more surely than if bars blocked their escape.

Paul's binding sat on him like a second skin, but like everything else it didn't matter. He didn't feel the despair that his fellow slaves exuded, nor did he wait eagerly for someone to tell him what to do next. Paul understood the slaves. They were the extreme result of people following the Book. They were so afraid of offending God that they were willing to sell their will so that any offense would fall on their owner. They traded away any responsibility for their lives.

Paul sat in a corner and let the motion of the boat move him. At first he'd tried to fight it, but it was like being a slave. He just let it happen and he stopped noticing it. Daniel had come down once and not returned. Paul had given him the Page.

"I don't need it," he'd said, "and I expect I won't be able to keep it. You hold onto it for now."

They'd been on the river for a week. The water was still fast, but it was mostly smooth now. It was easy to sit and wait. The first few minutes of the trip had been the scariest. The rest was boredom. He ate what they put in front of him and sat still the rest of the time. The distance between him and what happened to him was an abyss now. He could think about feelings, but it was too much work. It was easier to think of the mindless chores that filled his life before he was uprooted and sent out into the world.

Paul daydreamed about weeding his garden when he heard shouts from up on deck. A gentle bump shook them, then the captain opened the door.

"Welcome to Arik, slaves," he said. He didn't even look at Paul. Whatever misgivings he had were obviously gone. "Line up and follow the mate here to your new quarters."

The boat's mate waited until the captain had gone then he kicked the nearest slave. "Time to go," he shouted at them. Paul stood up and walked to the door and the rest followed him. He saw Daniel on the dock watching him. He thought about waving, but decided the mate wouldn't like it. When he looked again, Daniel was gone.

The quarters were rough but clean. There was water for drinking and washing and even short trousers for them to wear. The heat didn't bother Paul much more than the cold had. He drank some water and was careful to wash and put on clean clothes. He crouched in a corner of the room and felt his body gradually get accustomed to solid ground. In the evening someone brought in a large pot and some bowls. They were fed something that tasted like thin oatmeal.

Over the next few days people would wander into the compound and look at the slaves. Paul looked at them and they would shake their head and go to pick someone else.

"Keep your eyes down," the slave master said. "They don't like a slave that looks them in the eyes." Paul shrugged and kept his eyes down from then on. Still he was the last one in the compound when a young man in a black robe rushed in.

"I need a slave right away," he said to the slave master. "The Arch-Bishop's last one died from a bad mushroom."

"He's the only one left," the slave master said and pointed at Paul.

"I don't like the look of him."

"You can always tell the Arch-Bishop that you couldn't find one. Maybe he'll let you share his next meal."

"OK, I'll take him," the young man said, "but he better not be any trouble."

"Haven't had the least bit of trouble with him," the slave master said.

"Then why isn't he gone?"

"Does it matter if he is just a taster?"

"I guess not," the young man in the robe walked over to Paul. "Come on then." Paul stood up and followed the young man out of the compound.

The air outside was much warmer than in the compound and Paul wondered why the young man didn't fall over from the heat. He must be used to it, he thought. Rym in the North was made from grey stone, and this one from red, but the swarms of people were the same. Paul wondered how the rulers controlled the people here. He didn't see any ribbons or other badges and the clothes were a bewildering mix of colours. Instead of looking like a garden in spring it just looked garish.

The young man led him to a huge building covered with elaborate carvings. Paul looked at them with interest.

"This is the Cathedral. It is as grand as the Emperor's palace, and rightly so, as we do God's work." Paul just nodded. The young man shook his head. "Slaves," he said just loud enough for Paul to hear him. "You can't show them any kindness." He walked quickly through a large foyer to a small door. He opened the door and waved Paul through. "This is the back part of the Cathedral, where all the real work is down."

"I am sure the Bishop would be delighted to know that his efforts in the Cathedral pale beside the work you do. I'm sure God comes and dictates to you every night."

"Pfah," the young man said. "Brother John, you forget yourself."

"I may be a lowly brother," the man said and straightened his rough brown robe, "but I am the Bishop's lowly brother and I have his ear."

"Even the Bishop won't move against one of the Arch-Bishop's staff."

"Staff?" Brother John said. "You are barely a step above that slave you lead about and lecture like he cares where he is. If it weren't for him, you'd be tasting the Arch-Bishop's food yourself. I understand he still has a fondness for mushrooms."

The young man turned red, but instead of continuing the argument he led Paul deeper into the warren in the back half of the Cathedral. Paul could hear Brother John's laughter following them. They arrived at a stuffy corner and the young man pushed the door open.

"This is where you will stay unless I have need of you." The young man watched Paul sit on the bed. "I am Father Thom. If you get lost, ask for me."

"You are younger than Brother John," Paul said.

"I am ordained into orders. He is just a lay brother."

Paul didn't think Brother John thought of himself as just anything, but he didn't say so. The slave binding was making him even more detached. He sat on the bed as Father Thom left and closed the door behind him.

After some time a servant in grey clothes carried in a tray with two bowls and a larger covered dish. An armed guard watched with a bored expression.

The servant served something that looked like stew into the wooden bowl. Paul guessed that the other one belonged to the Arch-Bishop. He ate the food while the servant and the guard watched. When nothing happened, they left.

It was strange to be a slave in a small room and eat such rich food. Paul tasted things that he'd never thought of before. Some were so strange that he wondered if it was poisoned. He never spoke, and neither did the servant or the guard.

After he had been there for about a week, a Brother came to his room.

"What can you do besides eat?" he asked Paul.

"I'm a farmer," Paul said.

"Follow me." The Brother led him through the maze of hallways to a door. He threw the door open and led Paul out into the sunshine.

"There's a bucket, and the well," the Brother said pointing at each. "Water the plants. When you're finished, I'll take you back to your room."

"What's your name?" Paul asked.

"Oh, call me Brother Jude." The man walked away. Paul picked up the bucket and began watering the garden.

Every day, between tasting the Arch-Bishop's meals, Paul worked in the garden. He hauled water or pulled weeds. Sometimes he just swept the walks. They were all simple jobs, but they filled time and reminded him of home.

One day Father Thom found him in the garden.

"What are you doing here?" he said.

"Watering the garden," Paul said.

"Why?"

"It needs water."

Father Thom took a deep breath.

"Save your breath, Father, the slave binding makes them all a little dim." Brother Jude said as he came from the other side of the garden.

"I should have known it was you meddling."

"I don't like to see any waste. There's no reason why he can't be useful."

"Very well, but make sure he is there for the tasting."

Paul lost track of how long he alternated between the stuffy room and rich food and the simple work of the garden. He stopped paying attention to the food they served him. The flavours were too subtle for him.

One day he had the shakes after he finished the meal, but the servant and guard had already left. Paul thought about seeking out Father Thom to tell him, but he couldn't think how to explain why food that would kill the Arch-Bishop wouldn't kill him.

A different guard came that night and took Paul to a deep dark place and chained him to the wall.

"The Arch-Bishop is dead," Paul said.

"Yeah," the guard said, "he's dead, and you're alive and the Bishop is mighty curious how that happened." The guard turned and left Paul in the dark before Paul could think of a way to explain the impossible. He sat down and leaned against the cold stone wall. Paul hoped Daniel was in a better place.

Chapter 10

Daniel stood on the dock and watched Paul walk off the boat leading the other slaves. He shook with fear and anger, and he had no idea what to do. Daniel had never worried too much about the Book. Even if he glossed over some of the myriad of trivial instructions he still treasured the idea that God had given them the Book in order to keep them from displeasing God.

Now Paul said that he didn't think the Book was from God at all, and that the people who hurt others really were following their Book. Paul wanted to throw it all away and start doing everything that the Book said not to, but he was afraid. What if Paul was wrong?

He watched until the slaves had all disappeared into a functional looking building. Then he waited hoping that someone would go in and buy Paul and then Daniel could rescue him. Only nobody came and Daniel was getting hungry. He had no money and no way home, assuming he could rescue Paul. He needed help.

Paul had said that the Book was not from God. Yet God visited Paul and turned a page from Paul's Book into a Page. Now, it was time that Daniel ask that Page for help the way Paul did. The idea terrified him. The Page convinced Paul he needed to become a slave to get them to this city. Daniel didn't even know if Paul was certain the Sword they were looking for was here.

He pulled out the torn and bloody piece of paper. What he really wanted to do was burn it. Instead he carefully unfolded it and looked.

Chickens

It was so ridiculous that Daniel had to laugh. He stood there on the dock and laughed until tears ran down his face. Then the tears shifted, and he found himself kneeling on the dock hunched over and heaving huge wrenching sobs. His sides hurt and the noises that came out of him terrified him. He saw the constant passing of feet and legs of people who simply walked past him. Daniel felt alone and betrayed. How could God lead them to this place? He didn't know how long he knelt there, after the first wave of grief passed, clutching the Page.

A small hand tapped him on the shoulder.

"Hey mister," a young voice said, "are you OK?"

"I need to find chickens," Daniel's voice sounded like a croak to him.

"I know where you'll find some chickens." His new companion didn't appear to notice his disarray.

Daniel looked up and saw a small boy, or maybe a girl in a dusty robe. She, Daniel decided, it had to be a she, had soft brown eyes that were open wide in concern.

"That would be great," Daniel said, and he hiccuped. The little girl laughed and skipped off. Daniel scrambled to his feet and followed after. It was strange. The girl would skip along for a while, then meet another child and they would begin a spontaneous game of tag that would weave around Daniel. They met another group of children who were playing catch and threw the ball to the little girl. She caught it and tossed it back.

It was as if Daniel had been transported into an entirely different world. None of these children showed the slightest concern that they might displease God. They just played. None of the adults paid any attention to the children, and the children ignored the adults other than staying out from under foot. Daniel was caught in between.

Adults rushed about their business bumped and shoved him. Each had lines of worry and strain on their faces. They had the precepts of the Book to follow and horrible consequences if they displeased God. Daniel knew. He was a person of the Book, no matter how casually.

The children didn't know about the Book; they hadn't found it at the foot of their bed yet. Until they did, they would live carefree and entirely in the moment. It was a terrifying thought. At one time in Daniel's life he too must have lived without the Book. He tried to remember, but as hard as he tried he couldn't remember past the moment when he woke up to find the Book on the foot of his bed. How old was he then? Six, maybe seven?

The little girl skipped away from a game that involved throwing small stones into a circle in the dust. Adult feet carelessly erased the circle or kicked the stones away, but the children just laughed at the extra challenge and redrew the circle and tossed more stones. There were no real winners and no losers.

He almost lost the little girl in his fascination with the game. She came and tugged on his arm.

"Come on," she said. "We're almost there." She walked beside him holding his hand until they entered a huge open square that was filled with livestock of all descriptions.

"There are lots of chickens," the girl said, "but these are my favourites. They're the prettiest." A note of sadness entered her voice. "I think they're sick."

Daniel looked at the chickens in the cage in front of him. They were much fancier than his at home. These birds were in all the colours of the rainbow while his were just white and brown. He could see what the little girl meant; the chickens were listless and not moving around much, but the smell was rich and familiar. He felt the tears start up again and took a deep breath. He couldn't help Paul if he was weeping all the time.

"Hello, Sir." An adult man came up to stand beside Daniel. "Are you interested in one of these fine birds?" The little girl let go of Daniel's hand and ran off. She stopped once and waved at him, then vanished into the crowd.

"They're sick," Daniel said. "Doesn't your Book tell you how to care for them?"

"I'm a merchant, not a chicken farmer," the man said. "I'd hoped my son would get the Book for chicken farming, but he didn't. I don't think the birds are going to live much longer."

"I'm a chicken farmer back home," Daniel said. "These birds look very different from mine, but I think they need some gravel."

"Gravel?" the man said. "Why would they need gravel?"

"I have no idea." Daniel stooped to pick up some dust and let it run through his fingers. "But I have to make sure that my birds have access to the right kind of gravel."

"Joseph," the man shouted. A young boy came out of the tent that stood behind the chicken coop.

"Yes, Father," he said.

"This man says the chickens need gravel."

"Is that in his Book?" Joseph asked.

"Back home it is," Daniel said. The boy in front of him wasn't much older than the little girl, but he was already was developing the look of perpetual worry that Daniel knew was on his own face.

"When did you find your Book?" Daniel asked.

"Just last month," the boy said.

"Do you miss being a child and not having the Book?"

"What a strange question," Joseph's father said. "Do you?"

"I don't remember," Daniel admitted.

"I don't either," Joseph said. "Not really."

"Well Joseph, take Daniel and go buy some gravel."

"Yes, Father."

Daniel followed Joseph away through the livestock. Unlike the little girl, he walked as straight a line as the crowds allowed. His feet scuffed through circles and line in the dust and he ignored the laughter of the children. Daniel kept stopping to watch the children play, then rushed not to lose Joseph.

They found a man who sold gravel and Daniel picked out the stuff that seemed to be the right size. At least it would have been right back home. Joseph paid carefully with coins that weren't much different than what Daniel had seen in the north.

Joseph carried the gravel back to the chickens and Daniel scattered it in the coop. The birds pecked at it, so he hoped he'd guessed right.

"If this works," the man said, "I'll be in your debt."

"I could use a place to stay and food to eat," Daniel said.

"There is space in the tent behind the chickens. We live somewhere else and just come here to care for the birds."

"My name is Daniel."

"Albert," the man said and turned to look back at the birds. "Gravel, who would think gravel?"

Daniel went into the tent and sat down. It was warm and stuffy in there, but it was a place to stay. If Arik was anything like the Rym, it was dangerous to not have a place to retreat to.

Joseph came into the tent.

"If you want more air, you can tie the flap up," he said and demonstrated. "Father says that if you are hungry, you can join us for our evening meal."

"Thank you, Joseph."

The evening meal was a kind of stew with flat bread to eat with. Though it was very different from what Daniel was used to, he enjoyed it.

He spent his time either watching the chickens or watching the children at play. He really wanted to join in the game, but he was afraid to scare them. The little girl who had led him to the chickens stopped by and waved at him, but she didn't speak to him again.

Chapter 11

"What's it like having children?" Daniel asked Albert one day as they watched the much improved chickens peck at the gravel and feed in the dust at the bottom of their cage.

"It's a terrifying time until they get their Book," Albert said. "There's no telling what they might do. I came home one day to find that Joseph had painted an entire wall with pictures of animals."

"So he likes animals. That's good, isn't it?"

"He got the Book for numbers or something. It has to do with adding things in columns. Joseph says it will be very helpful for the business. I was so relieved when he got his Book and I could predict what he would do. Before that, the Book said not to see what the children do, but it is hard not to worry."

Daniel went to the slave market to check on Paul, but he found the place was empty. He went back to the livestock market and watched the children play. This wasn't getting him any closer to learning about the Sword or where Paul was. Albert had taken to avoiding him, but Joseph would come and stand and watch the chickens with Daniel.

"I think we will make a little money on the birds," Joseph said. "The gravel made them a bit more expensive, but at least we didn't lose any. I'm trying to decide what price to put on them."

"Have you checked what other people are selling chickens for?"

"Yes, but the plain ones are much cheaper than we can afford to sell these for. No one else has such fancy birds."

"That should make them more valuable then."

"I hope so," Joseph sighed and tossed some feed into the coop. "It would be nice to be able to ask the Sword."

"The Sword?" Daniel tried to keep the eagerness out of his voice.

"Our Emperor rules Arik with a Sword that tells the Truth. If I could ask it about my price for the chickens it would tell me whether it was a true price."

"I see," Daniel said. "Does the Emperor allow people to ask questions?"

"Sort of," Joseph said. "If you can pay, sometimes you can ask. The Truth is supposed to cost something."

"I suppose he uses it at other times to solve problems?"

"I don't know. He's the Emperor. He has the Book for being Emperor, so he can't be wrong. He just says what's to happen and people do it. They don't want him needing to use the Sword."

"Why not?"

"They say that not only does the Truth cost, but it hurts."

"Ah," Daniel nodded like he knew what Joseph was talking about, but he thought this Sword sounded a lot like the Cauldron. It might have started as one thing, but changed into something different.

He went back to the slave market again. Maybe if he found someone he could learn where Paul had been taken. This time he found a young man sweeping the compound.

"Sorry, we don't have any slaves today," the young man said. "The boat should be coming in this week."

"My friend was sold as a slave," Daniel said. "I was hoping to find him and see if he's OK."

"Waste of time, that." The young man stopped his sweeping to look at Daniel. "The slave binding makes them slow, and it gets worse as time goes on. It isn't like slaves need to think for themselves. So your friend might still be alive, but it isn't like he'll still be himself. Just go home and forget about him. It's for the best."

Daniel wandered away taking random turns depending on the crowd. Following the spaces in the crowd brought him to the steps of a huge building. He wondered if it was the King's palace, but there were few guards and people streamed in and out of the massive doors. Daniel walked up the stairs and through the door.

The crowd flowed through another set of doors and entered an immense space. Daniel could barely see the ceiling in the gloom. Though candles were everywhere they seemed to cast as much shadow as light.

There was someone up front speaking from a high platform.

"...our duty as creations of God is to live our lives so as to not displease our creator. *We entreat thee, O God, to tell us how we might live to not offend you.* Following the Book is only a beginning of righteous. *We entreat thee, O God, to tell us how we might live to not offend you.* We need to give up all desire, all thought and become one with the Book. *We entreat thee, O God, to tell us how we might live to not offend you.* Only when we have emptied ourselves completely will we be worthy of God."

"What is this place?" Daniel said. People around him turned and hushed him. The hiss spread across the vast room like the sound of wind in leaves. A young woman in the row in front of him turned around. She recognized Daniel in the same moment that he recognized her.

"Why, hello, Grounds Keeper," the Master's daughter said. "This is the Cathedral, the centre of our faith. Here God is entreated night and day to have mercy on his creatures and guide us in what we should do." She gave a predatory smile. "I know what I am being guided to do." She crooked a finger at him and Daniel found his legs lifting him up and carrying him toward her. She took his hand in hers and pulled him toward the side of the Cathedral.

"The Arch-Bishop is dead!" someone shouted from a balcony high above the crowd. "He was poisoned! The Choosers have murdered God's man!"

There was a wail from the gathered crowd and the man who was speaking stumbled momentarily. The Master's daughter looked away for a moment and the compulsion on Daniel weakened. He wrenched himself away from her and went running out of the Cathedral. He was followed by a stream of people who cried out that Choosers were among them. The city was doomed!

Much of the crowd melted into the city spreading panic and despair, but a small portion obviously had a goal. They bowled people over as they made their way. Daniel decided to follow them. It was better than being lost in a city given over to panic. He ran in the vacuum left behind the group he followed. It helped that the streets here were wide and not as crowded as the rest of Arik. It reminded him of the area the Master lived in Rym. The area where Paul and Daniel had lived until the Master's daughter began using Daniel to fill her own cruel needs.

What was she doing here? Daniel had thought her too young to travel so far on her own, but he hadn't seen any sign of anyone else. Her reaction to Daniel in the Cathedral was certainly not of a girl who needed to be circumspect around her father.

He arrived in a large square that was in front of a building that was even larger than the Cathedral. This had to be the Emperor's palace. People were standing in front of the gates while guards held them back and others ran to reinforce them.

A man in a rich black robe walked out of the castle and strolled up to the gate.

"My people," he said in a tenor voice that carried all the way to Daniel at the back of the crowd, "my people, I have just heard of this tragedy. As your Bishop, you know that there is no one who loved the Arch-Bishop more than I. I will be advising the Emperor to use the full power of the Sword to learn what truth to tell you."

People started shouting for the Emperor. Daniel wanted to stay and see the Emperor and maybe this Sword he'd heard about, but he saw someone walk up beside the Bishop. He recognized the Master's daughter. She was looking through the crowd for something, or someone. Daniel turned and fled.

Chapter 12

It was chilly in the cell. Paul leaned his head back against the wall and let the coolness flow through him. They had poisoned him six times now and used stronger poison each time. Paul figured they wanted to know who had poisoned the Arch-Bishop, but he couldn't tell them. He didn't know.

He heard Father Thom over a cell or two. The Father was quiet now, but at first time he had addressed God with a constant petition to hear him and tell him how not to offend. It had jarred Paul's nerves, and he was certain that it was jarring to God as well. When Father Thom fell silent Paul was relieved.

As he sat in the dark, Paul realized there was something wrong with him. Ever since he had drained the Cauldron for God, nothing had really touched him. He felt pain and cold, he even felt pity for Father Thom, but it didn't connect to anything. It didn't matter. The pain couldn't kill him, nor the cold, nor the pity.

Paul had survived the impossible, but he didn't care. Somehow his capacity to care about the things that flowed through him had broken. The only thing that troubled him at all was Daniel. He wondered where he was, and what he was doing. He was sorry that he'd brought Daniel along, even though God had made Daniel his companion. Paul thought Daniel had a very poor return for being Paul's companion.

Guards came and dragged Paul out of his cell. He caught a glimpse of a body in a black robe lying flaccid on a cell floor. So Father Thom was dead. No wonder he'd stopped talking. They strapped him to a table and stood back.

"If we are going to question him properly," a male voice said from out of sight of Paul, "we must remove the slave binding."

"That will be too dangerous," a different man protested.

"He is chained to a table that is bolted to the floor. He may have a capacity to survive poison, but unless he is able to break the chains, he is trapped here. I have information that suggests that he is no stronger than any of you."

"Very well, Your Eminence," the second man said, "though I'm not sure this will work." He stepped up to where Paul could see him holding the glass bead that contained Paul's blood. The slave binding. Using a knife the man broke the glass and let the blood drip onto Paul.

Paul didn't feel any different, but then he hadn't felt much of the original binding.

"Now," the Bishop said, leaning over Paul, "what should we call you, ex-slave?"

"Paul."

"Very good, Paul."

"Tell me about the Arch-Bishop's death. How did the Choosers get to him?"

"I don't know anything about Choosers."

"No?" The Arch-Bishop peered at him. "Not even though you are a notorious Chooser yourself and your friend is lose in the city to spread the cancer of the heresy?"

"I have no idea what you are talking about."

"No, but given enough time, you will." The Bishop patted Paul's cheek. "You will."

"Put him to the question," he ordered them. "Give him a rest whenever he speaks the truth we desire to hear."

"Yes, Your Eminence."

The Bishop left and the rest of the guards started to work on Paul.

The process of torture was strange. Paul felt the pain and wanted it to stop, but it didn't matter enough for him to bother learning what they wanted him to learn. After a while they gave up and left him alone.

He was sleeping in the dark when a light touch run down his chest.

"So many scars!" a familiar voice said. "How does he survive?"

Paul opened his eyes to see the Master's daughter and the Bishop standing over him.

"How it happened is less important than the fact that it happened." The Bishop slapped at the woman's hand. "Stop playing with him. It's distracting."

"His friend is more fun anyway."

"It was your games that got us into this trouble."

"Did you find the Page that the King babbled about?"

"No, he must have given it to his friend."

"So when his friend comes to me, he will bring the Page."

"The binding is gone."

"The binding from the Cauldron is gone. I put a different kind of binding on him. When I am ready, he will come."

"Like he followed you at the Cathedral?"

"He'll come."

The Bishop picked up a spike and examined it carefully. Then he drove it down into Paul's chest. The spike hurt in a distant way and his heart fluttered as it tried to beat around the steel intruder. When the Bishop removed the spike the wound closed up and Paul's heart took up its beat.

"Curious," the Bishop said. "I thought the King had exaggerated; obviously not."

"Paul," the Bishop said, "we are serpentines. We are the true rulers of this world."

"The Book."

"Yes, the Book," the Bishop said. "You are so grateful when we offer to guide you so that you won't offend God. You soak it all in, no matter how trivial we made it. You do anything we tell you, as long as we tell you it is to avoid displeasing God. Do you ever wonder what God must think of you?"

"I think God must be sad."

"Not the word I was thinking of," the Bishop said. "I think you got a glimpse of the reality we've shaped when you took the Cauldron. We still don't know how you managed that. But nonetheless, I think it made you very nearly one of us."

"We could take you the rest of the way," the Master's daughter said. "You could rule the world with us."

"All we want to know is who is helping you," the Bishop said.

"God," Paul said. "He came to visit me in my kitchen."

"Impossible!" the Bishop shouted.

"Try again," the Master's daughter said. "There must be a serpentine playing its own game with the world. Who is helping you?"

"God," Paul said again.

The Bishop snarled and slammed the spike into Paul again.

"If we leave it there long enough," he said, "maybe even you will die."

He took his companion's arm and led her out of the dungeon.

Paul's heart refused to stop beating no matter how much he asked it to.

The guard and his helpers were horrified to find Paul with the spike through his heart. They were even more horrified to find that he was still alive. They used a pry bar to remove it, but then couldn't decide what to do next.

"How can we torture someone who can survive being nailed to the table?" one asked.

They left him in the dark. Paul hoped the Bishop wasn't too hard on them for removing the spike.

The Bishop returned alone. He stood by Paul's head in the dim torture chamber.

"I should introduce myself, Paul," the Bishop said. "I am Beelphael, and my lovely companion is Seepharel. We are older than this world. There are others here and there, but they are lesser. We are the eldest, the most powerful. Imagine us, inviting you to join us. All we need is for you to give your loyalty to us."

"I don't like you," Paul said. "You've made the world a cruel and comfortless place."

"Join us and you can shape the world anyway you want to. Come now, Paul, you have the chance to make the first real decision of your entire life."

"You're right," Paul said, "I need to make a decision. I'm deciding against you."

"You're a fool," Beelphael said. "You may be immortal. Can you imagine spending eternity on this table?"

He left Paul alone.

<u>Chapter 13</u>

Daniel sat in his tent and shook. She was after him. Somehow she was connected with the Bishop and she knew he was here. He felt her pull on him, even from this tent.

Joseph came into the tent and tied up the flaps.

"It's stuffy in here," he said. "Everybody's talking about the Choosers. That's kids' talk."

"Kids' talk?" Daniel said. "Tell me about it."

Joseph looked confused for a moment, "What was I saying?" he said, "I have to go read my Book." He ran out of the tent.

Daniel followed him out, but Joseph had vanished in the crowds. The people gathered in clumps. Wild speculation bounded from one group to another. The only people who weren't affected were the children. They still played and ran through the market.

Daniel walked out into the market and looked for the girl who'd led him to the chickens. She was playing tag with some other children. Daniel sat down and watched them.

"May I play?" he asked as the little girl ran past.

"Don't you have a Book?" she said.

"I left it at home."

"But you helped the chickens."

"I like chickens."

"So, do I. Tag, you're it." She ran away screaming and Daniel chased after her. The children ran easily between the adults and Daniel had to constantly twist and turn to avoid knocking people over. They frowned at him and pointed fingers. Then, between one step and the next, Daniel stopped worrying about the adults and his problems and his questions and he just played the game. He managed to tag a little boy, who laughed in delight and ran off after another child. Daniel ran and played through the square. He stopped to throw pebbles at a circle in the dust and laughed with the children at how bad a shot he was.

Daniel played until he was so tired that he just fell to the dust, laughing. He couldn't remember the last time he felt so good. Yes, he could. He had been playing tag with Paul and Diana. They had run naked through the summer heat until sweat had coated them and they glistened in the sun. Then they had rolled in the dust until they were the same colour as the dirt. They finished by jumping into the water. The cool water cleansed them and made them laugh even louder.

"Who wants to play Choosers?" Diana had said.

"Who wants to play Choosers?" the little girl said as she sat herself on Daniel's stomach.

Daniel felt himself split. Part of him swam in the river back home; a child with no care or Book. The other part lay in the dust listening to the children hoping that he would learn an answer to a question he didn't know how to ask.

> *"Adam in the Garden,*
> *so very sad is he,*
> *can't pick the apple*
> *from God's Tree.*
> *Eve in the evening*
> *weeping in the night,*
> *afraid she'll get God angry*
> *if she takes a bite.*
> *What makes God happy?*
> *What makes God sad?*
> *Be foolish or wise*
> *But choose you must!"*

All the children chanted and Daniel found himself chanting along. When they got to the "choose you must!" the little girl pointed at each child who was nearby.

"Candy!" yelled one.

"A dog!" yelled another.

"Mom!" said a third.

"Chickens!" said the little girl, and she pointed at Daniel.

"Children," Daniel said and all the children laughed.

"You win," the little girl said and gave him a wet little child kiss on the cheek.

The children ran away laughing, but Daniel lay on ground and remembered. Paul and Diana and he had played that game a lot. They always chose different things; sometimes to make the others laugh, sometimes just what they wanted, but always a choice. It was what they wanted at that exact moment in time. Children were all Choosers before the Book made them afraid.

"Sir, are you alright?" a man looked down at Daniel with a concerned expression.

"Just a dizzy spell," Daniel said.

"You need some water," the man said. "It's been too much excitement, learning that the Choosers are among us."

"That's true enough." Daniel let the man help him to his feet and take him to his booth where he plied Daniel with water.

"Are you sure you're alright now?" the man asked when Daniel stood to leave.

"Yes, I think so," Daniel said. "I really do think so."

He walked through the gathering dusk and heard parents calling children in for supper and bed. He remembered that now too. As much as he wished he could return forever to the days of his childhood and its complete lack of care and burden, he couldn't. What he did have was the knowledge that he could choose. The call from the Master's daughter was still there, but he wasn't going to follow it. Not yet, not until he was ready.

The next day the market was still abuzz with speculation about the Arch-Bishop's death.

"It seems very strange that they have caught someone and we haven't seen him questioned with the Emperor's Sword," Daniel said in one group.

"How do we know it really is the Choosers if the Emperor's Sword doesn't test them?" he said in another.

"The Emperor's Sword has the power to show the truth," he said in a third. "Why doesn't he use it?"

It wasn't long before he started hearing his own words coming back at him. He wandered through Arik and listened. Everywhere he didn't hear people talking about the Sword, he put in a comment then moved on.

The crowd took on a life of its own. People were chanting at the Emperor's Palace asking the Emperor to use his Sword to save them.

After two days, a representative of the Emperor came out to say that the Chooser would be put to the test of the Sword at the Cathedral square at noon. Daniel was at the edge of the crowd when the announcement was made. He started to follow the link to the Master's daughter.

The link's faint trail led him to the Cathedral, where a large crowd already gathered. Daniel edged his way along until he was up against a wall. He could barely see the steps. It was good enough.

The Master's daughter wasn't far away. the pull on his gut was faint, but it never stopped. He wondered if she felt his presence. It didn't matter; he was sure that wherever she was, Paul would be close by. He was there for Paul, not for her.

Chapter 14

Seerpharel stroked Paul's scars.

"I could teach you so much," she said, "We could have such pleasure." She dragged a knife along the line of the scar, "Or maybe it's pain you prefer."

"Seerpharel, I don't think you're achieving anything." Beelphael said. "The people are demanding the Emperor put him to the Sword."

"He can't do that," she snapped. "We have no idea what would happen."

"The Emperor is saying he is bound by the Book to do so."

"Tell him not to."

"I can't tell him to ignore the Book."

"Then change the Book."

"Do you really want him to know the part of the Book that makes him Emperor can be changed?"

There was a knock on the door.

"The Emperor wishes the prisoner to be brought out for questioning."

"Very well," Beelphael said. "Make sure that he is well secured. He's a dangerous man."

"Yes, Your Eminence."

The guard wrapped Paul up in so many chains that he couldn't lift his arms or move his legs. They loaded him on a trolley and fastened the chains to it. The guards didn't take the stairs up, but rather a long spiraling ramp. They moved like they were accustomed to the trolley and its weight of chain. The ramp ended at a wooden door in the wall that was just big enough for the trolley to fit through.

Through the door was sunshine and the murmuring of a huge crowd. Paul was lying on his back so the sun glared straight into his eyes. He was trundled along to where a hook dangled from a scaffold above. The guards quickly hooked his chains to that hook and somewhere Paul heard a wheel and a ratchet. The chains tightened and gradually lifted him off the trolley until he hung suspended above the pavement. Other than his complete lack of freedom it wasn't unpleasant. The chains supported him comfortably and Paul was able to feel the warmth of the sun for the first time in days.

A man in fine gold clothes and surrounded by guards in black walked up to Paul. He poked at Paul and set him swinging gently.

"Is this him?" he said.

"Yes, Your Majesty," the head guard said.

"I've heard that he is immune to poison."

"It appears to be so."

"And to torture?"

"That may be true too."

"Then what should we do with him," the Emperor shouted and turned to the crowd.

"The Sword, the Sword!" they shouted.

"Do you think he might be immune to the Sword?" the Emperor asked the crowd.

"Never!" they thundered.

He drew a sword from a scabbard on his belt and held it in front of Paul.

"Do you know what this is?" he asked.

"A sword."

"It is THE Sword," the Emperor said. "The Sword that reveals truth. The Sword that maintains justice in our city. Speak the Truth and the Truth will set you free."

The Emperor put the Sword up in front of Paul's eyes.

"Were you the Arch-Bishop's slave?" The Emperor asked in a thundering voice.

"I was," Paul said.

"Did you eat his food?"

"I did."

"Did you know he was poisoned?"

"I did."

"But you didn't die."

"Poison can't kill me."

There were gasps from the crowd.

"They put you to the question?"

"Yes."

"What did you tell them?"

"Nothing," Paul said, trying to project his voice further into the crowd. "Torture doesn't touch me either."

There were louder gasps and a rolling murmur ran through the square.

"But you know the truth?"

"I do."

"You know who murdered our Arch-Bishop."

"I do. He is called Beelphael, but you don't know him by that name."

"What name do I know him by?"

"The Bishop."

There were screams and shouts in the crowd. The Emperor looked confused and peered at the Sword as if it wasn't doing what it was supposed to.

"You're lying!" he said. "You have to be lying."

"No," Paul said. "The truth is that we all live a lie."

"No!" the Emperor said. He pushed the Sword against Paul's eyes. "Tell me a lie, prove to me that the Sword still works."

"God wrote your Book." The Sword burst into blue flame, and turned Paul's eyes to ash in an instant.

"But that is the truth," the Emperor screamed. "God did write the Books." The heat of the Sword on his skin increased and he smelled burning flesh, the Sword had started to burn the Emperor. The Emperor shrieked even louder while the crowd broke into chaos.

The Emperor must have panicked, because Paul felt a fiery pain as the Sword cut through the chains and skewered him just below his ribs. The fire consumed him and yet it didn't. Paul saw the world in chiaroscuro; everything light or dark. Truth or lie. He looked at his own life and saw the lie in his desire to not offend God. It was his fear that drove him to follow the Book; pride that sent him out on his quest.

It wasn't something broken in him that disconnected him from the pain of torture or the cold of winter. It was fear that his emotions would fail him. That he would displease God because he was a failure, a fraud. After a lifetime of avoiding himself, he was afraid to do something, anything, that might tip a balance against him.

He was destroying his world, and he was afraid to live in the world that resulted. Paul wept bitterly. As the tears ran down his face, the flames began to flicker out and his eyes to grow back. Just as the flames vanished he caught a glimpse of a face. It was creased, not with displeasure, but with sorrow. Then his sight returned and the first thing he saw was Daniel looking at him.

"I think we should get out of here before somebody comes to their senses and tries to tie you up again."

"Very well," Paul said. "Lead on."

Paul followed Daniel to a large market filled with livestock. It was empty except for some children who were playing, unconcerned in the sun.

"You will have to teach your parents the Choosing Game," Daniel said to a little girl.

"Silly," she said. "They won't listen."

"I did," Daniel said. "Someone might."

The little girl shrugged and said, "OK," then ran off to play with the others.

"What was that about?" Paul asked.

"I'll tell you about it on the walk."

"Walk?"

"I'm not letting you get on a boat again. It's time to go home.

"So we're walking?"

"We walk." Daniel pointed vaguely north. "That way."

<u>Chapter 15</u>

The dust of the trail coated them, even though they were only a stone's throw from the river. It reminded Paul of the tang of the dust on the first day of their quest. His heart ached at how eager and foolish he'd been then.

He looked at Daniel. at least his friend found something to treasure on this last part of their trip. He seemed younger, or older, maybe wiser. Paul couldn't put his finger on it. Something happened, something to do with the game that Daniel kept trying to teach him.

That game, Paul shook his head, he had no idea what it was about. Daniel wanted him to choose what his heart wanted in the instant of asking. The problem was that life was too complicated. Paul couldn't narrow it down to one thing. It always had ifs or maybes about it. He shook his head and watched his friend crouch down to peer at something beside the trail; a rock most likely. If Daniel pointed his finger and said choose right now, Paul might just say whatever it was that Daniel had found. For a second, he caught a glimpse of a possibility, then his stomach rumbled.

"Hey, Daniel," Paul shouted, "Is whatever you're looking at edible? I'm hungry."

"You're always hungry," Daniel said as he stood up. "What happened to not needing food?"

"My body doesn't need food to live," Paul said, "but I need food to stay connected to life." Daniel had as much trouble understanding Paul's reconnection to the things of life as Paul had with Daniel's game.

"I think there must be another village up ahead," Daniel said. "We can get some water and supplies there."

"And what makes you think that there is a village ahead?"

"That would be the goat poop that you wanted to eat." Daniel grinned at Paul and he couldn't help but grin back.

"So explain again, about this game," Paul said.

"The children play it," Daniel said, "before they find the Book. We used to play it when we were children."

"So you've told me, but I can't remember anything before finding the Book."

"Neither could I until I started playing with the children. Something happened, and I just forgot to think about anything, then it all came back."

"I'm sure that you're right and it is very important." Paul kicked a stone and watched it skip ahead throwing up little dust clouds. "Actually, I think it is the most important thing we've learned yet. I just don't know what to do with it."

"I'm trying to get the children to teach the adults in each village."

"I've seen that. Have you had any better luck than with that first girl?"

"Not really. The children live in their own world. It barely touches the one the adults live in. Albert sounded as if, as a father, he couldn't wait for his son to get the Book and he could stop worrying about what Joseph was doing."

"Yet we are still here."

"Yeah, we are."

"No, think about it. In all the generations since the Garden, not one child has displeased God."

"How many generations has it been anyway?"

"I have no idea," Paul said, "People used to say that my great-grandfather claimed to walk with God every day. He was named after his great-grandfather, or maybe it was a great-great who was supposed to be Adam's great grandson."

"So how many greats is that?"

"I don't know, I keep losing count."

"Whatever number it is, the children all seem to pass on the Choosing Game to the younger ones. It probably goes right back to Adam's children."

"Maybe. What will happen in Eben?" Paul asked. "I don't recall seeing any children there."

"Have you seen children in any village before I pointed them out?" Daniel said, and laughed. "There is something in the Book that doesn't want us remembering, or even seeing children."

"Strange."

"Look, there's the village," Daniel said. "You can eat while we play."

Paul sat and ate the bread the villagers gave them and watched Daniel play with the children. The adults came and talked to him, but it was like Daniel was invisible. Paul looked on wistfully. The play called to something deep inside of him, but he didn't know how to let it out.

They helped repair some houses and clean out the well in repayment for the food that they were given. None of the villages seemed concerned about what was happening in the rest of the world. The Books they had were slim volumes in comparison to Paul's Book that he had left behind. They rarely opened them and they didn't have much of the constant worry that Paul saw in the cities.

Yet the Books were there, and the children were still masked from sight.

Close to a month later they walked into Brurn, and immediately heard rumour and speculation about what had happened in Arik to the south.

"The Choosers corrupted the Cathedral."

"The Arch-Bishop was poisoned. He was a Chooser in disguise."

"No it was the Bishop who was in disguise."

"The Emperor got burned up by his own Sword."

"He was an impostor. That's why he was burned."

"There were two creatures watching the whole thing. When the Sword lit up in flames, they flew away. I was there and saw the whole thing."

Paul looked at Daniel and raised his eyebrows.

"Don't look at me," Daniel said. "I was watching you. I just followed her to make sure it was really you they brought out."

"I wouldn't be surprised if they did fly," Paul said. "They are ancient and powerful creatures."

"They might have been lying to you."

"They probably were," Paul agreed. "But if they've really been running the world all this time, then there is some truth in their words."

They walked up the road toward Cepha. It wasn't long before they would be home. Paul wasn't sure what he would do when he got there.

Like Brurn, Cepha was in turmoil over the events to the South.

"With all this going on," an old man said as they helped him stack his firewood, "you'd think that someone had gone and eaten the apple."

"What's wrong with apples?" asked Paul.

"Not an apple, the apple," the old man said, "the Fruit from God's Tree that started all this fuss."

"It's an apple?" asked Daniel.

"Nah, it looks a little like one, but it's different too."

"You've seen the Fruit?" Paul said.

"The Book sends two a generation, one man and one woman to gaze on the Fruit of the forbidden tree. It just looked like an apple. Never could stand apples."

"So you know where the Garden is."

"Nope. Why would I want to know that? They took us east a ways and there was some secret village. They blindfolded us and carried us for days before they let us see. We were in the Garden then. Pretty spot. Never did have a taste for apples though. Then they brought us home."

Paul finished stacking the wood in silence.

"Let me guess," Daniel said. "We're heading east."

Chapter 16

"I am going east," Paul said. "You are going home."

"Ask me to Choose and I will say at the side of my friend," Daniel said.

"Ask me and I would say that my friend is safe."

"I won't feel right," Daniel said, "if I am safe, and you are lost."

Paul sighed. "Very well," he said, "we go east."

They spent the coin they had earned working for people around Cepha on food.

"You heading out again?" the bread maker said as he packed the loaves in their bag.

"Going east," Paul said.

"There's nothing east," the man said.

"Then I guess we'll find nothing," Daniel said.

"You can go west to Brurn and the River and south to Arik, or take that little path and walk to Eben. You can risk the path north and go to Rym, but you can't go east."

There was no break in houses on the east side of the square so they went to the north road. As soon as they reached the forest they turned to the right and pushed through the brush. The branches caught and held them. Roots tripped them, but they persevered. Finally the forest started opening up. Soon it was easy to walk and they were making good time. Toward evening they stumbled onto a path. As they stepped on the path the ground under their feet shifted and they fell to their knees.

When they could stand again Paul could see lights ahead. His heart sunk as they walked toward the lights. He could see from here that they had returned to Cepha.

They tried the next day from the path south and ended up on the road to Rym.

"Well," Paul said, "we've learned something."

"What's that?" Daniel said as he picked burrs from his clothes.

"There is something to the east, and someone doesn't want us to find it."

"That's helpful."

"It is," Paul said. "We're on the right track."

"We just can't stay on it."

"What did the old man say? That they came and took him east. Maybe we can't go there ourselves, maybe we have to be taken there."

"So who would be able to take us if we can't find the path. It doesn't seemly humanly possible."

"No, but it would be possible for a serpentine."

"I don't want anything to do with either of those two."

"No, you're right about that. They're too powerful, but they talked about other, younger serpentines. They as much as told me I could be one if I helped them."

"They were lying."

"Of course they were," Paul said, "but all the best lies start with the truth."

"So where do we go?"

"I don't know, but I'm wondering about Rym. We didn't see much of that city. If Arik had a Cathedral, I wonder if Rym has one too, or something similar."

"Oh great," Daniel said, "at worst we can be foresters again."

They rose in the morning and stretched then went to see if they had money for food to get to Rym.

"Funny you should ask," the baker said. "Cooran is putting together a wagon to go to Rym. The Book says that the place has opened up to trade again. He might appreciate having a couple of guys who've been there to show him the ropes."

They found Cooran checking the goods on the wagon. He was a nervous man only a few years older than Paul.

"It's strange. The Book sending me to Rym," he said. "It's always been Brurn."

"Not trading slaves?" Daniel said.

"No, don't know where the slaves come from. North along the river maybe. There's towns and villages enough there." He gave the straps a last tug. "I hope they like wool, up there. I have a whole wagon load of nothing but wool and sheepskin."

"I think you'll be fine." Daniel said. "The ones we ran into liked the sheepskin well enough."

"Let's get going then."

The wagon rolled through the forest without any problem. Paul and Daniel cleared the few trees that still lay across the road, but most of the trees had been sawn up and hauled away.

"Lots of changes," Daniel said as they walked past the clearing where the massive tree had lain across the road.

"Let's hope that some of them are for the good," Paul said.

The line up to get into Rym wasn't any shorter, but they were no longer handing out ribbons. Instead armed guards patrolled the streets.

"Let's find a market," Daniel said. Paul watched him go still; his friend was watching children at play. Now that he knew they were there, he could see them too. It was weird how an entire world was unnoticed by the adults most of the time. Daniel talked to a little boy who pointed away up the road and made some swinging motions with his arm, then held his nose.

"So?" Paul asked, when Daniel came back.

"This way," Daniel said. "I just hope the King isn't looking out his bathroom window. The road goes past the back wall of the palace."

They walked through Rym with the wagon following them. There was plenty of time to look around. Most people still wore the ribbons, but Paul saw a woman with a grey ribbon arguing with a man wearing a red. The compulsion was gone; it was just habit that remained.

The back wall of the palace had no windows and it seemed to roll on forever. Eventually it disappeared and they entered a maze of streets.

"The boy said when we got lost to stop and sniff."

Paul took a deep breath. "There seems to be an odd smell coming from that way." They followed the smell which gradually changed from odd, to bad, to horrific. Far from disconcerting the wool merchant, the reek made him happy.

"Dyers," he said, "they smell almost as much as tanners."

"If you don't mind," Paul said, "We will leave you here. Our noses aren't accustomed to the odours of your trade."

"Fine, fine. Thanks for your help." The trader led his wagon away with his nose in the air as a guide.

"So which way do we go?" Daniel asked.

"Away from the stink," Paul said.

They found the back wall of the palace again, but Daniel led them into a tiny square.

"I heard the children playing," he said.

Paul and Daniel stood and watched the game. Paul was amazed at how both the adults and the children moved their own way in their own time and yet never collided. After a bit Daniel kicked a stone into one of the circles the children had drawn. The children laughed and went back to their games. He kicked another stone and again the children laughed. The third time a small girl came up and stared at him.

"You want to play?" she asked.

"Come on, Paul," Daniel said and he ran into the square. They played tag, and Daniel was as agile as the children, and as unnoticed. Paul wanted to join them; to run and laugh without a care in the world. His feet stayed anchored to the pavement though a smile played across his face.

Dusk was falling when Daniel came back to Paul.

"Why didn't you join us?"

"I'm not sure," Paul said. "It wasn't that I didn't want to. I guess I'm not ready."

"It took me a while too," Daniel said. "We'll make a child of you yet."

Paul laughed and they wandered out of the square.

"The children said there's a park this way with an old shed we can sleep in."

"They are a fountain of information."

"The children play all over the city, and they notice things. It's a matter of not asking the right questions."

"Not asking?"

"If you ask directly it doesn't seem to work. They start thinking about what they're telling you and it gets muddled. I just talk about what I wish for, and all kinds of things pour out and it's a matter of sifting through and using what I need."

They found the park and the shed. It looked like it was going to fall over at any minute, but Paul figured it would stand for a few more nights. The weather was warm enough now that they only needed it to stay out of sight of the guards.

In the morning they went in search of the Library, which Daniel learned was covered with pretty pictures and was full of books that anyone could look at.

The Library was a painted story book. They spent most of the morning walking around following the different tales.

"I was thinking that the world was without redemption, then I see something like this," Paul said.

"It must be old," Daniel said.

"Oh yes," said a quavering voice beside them. "It is the oldest building left in the city. My grandfather used to bring me here after I found my Book. The world is larger than our Books he used to say."

"A wise man," Paul said to the old woman.

"Wiser, than I deserved," the old woman said. "I never brought my children here. The Book didn't say so, and so I didn't. Forgot about it until now." She wandered away. Paul and Daniel started watching the crowd. People walked in and out of the Library, but only the very young and a few very old people looked at the paintings on its walls.

"If adults can't see the pictures," Paul said, "there is something in them we need to see." They walked quicker and peered harder at the walls, but the stories faded and twisted until they were impossible to follow.

"Wait," Paul said. "We're losing it. What changed?"

"We changed," Daniel said. "We started looking for answers instead of just seeing the stories. Just admire the pictures, don't try to understand them."

Gradually Paul could see the vibrant colours again. Daniel would laugh and point to an animal or a funny scene and Paul would see and laugh too. They meandered back and forth without any plan or purpose other than the enjoyment of the stories. Late in the afternoon, Paul saw a picture of two children holding hands in a forest. There was a tree in front of them covered with golden fruit.

"Children," Paul said in a whisper. "They take children to the Garden."

<u>Chapter 17</u>

"It makes sense," Daniel said, "If it really is a testing of humanity it would have to be by someone who had never read the Book."

Paul leaned against the wall of the shed and thought.

"I think you're right," he said, "but I don't understand why. What is the purpose of making a child choose whether to eat or not eat from God's Tree."

"What if this is all about the Tree and the Garden?" Daniel said. "The serpentines got us out of the Garden by promising us the Book and a way to be sure that we didn't make God angry. It might not be the serpentines who bring the children to the Garden."

"So why are we here?" Paul said. "We could have asked a child and we'd be further ahead."

"I don't think so," Daniel said. "The old man said that it was once in a generation. I haven't heard about any games that talk about the Garden."

"Adam in the Garden,
so very sad is he,
can't pick the apple
from God's Tree.
Eve in the evening
weeping in the night,
afraid she'll get God angry
if she takes a bite.
What makes God happy?
What makes God sad?
Be foolish or wise
But choose you must!"

Daniel pointed to Paul and he said without thinking "Home."

"Home."

"The Garden is home," Daniel said. "It's where we started. I wonder if every child lives just a little bit in the Garden.

"That makes sense, but I don't know how it will help."

"Let's go back to the Library in the morning," Daniel said. "Maybe we will learn something else."

They returned to the Library, but the stories they saw changed.

"I don't know how it changed," Daniel said.

"We've changed again," Paul said. "so we've changed the stories."

"If we change the stories, how do we know they're true?"

"When I took in the Cauldron," Paul said, "I took in the life that it contained. Perhaps when I took the Sword I also gained the ability to see the truth." He breathed deeply and imagined himself back in the chains. Trapped by his lies and the lies of those around him. The flame of the Sword burned through the lies and left only the truth, but the truth burned. The light was painful as it illuminated the places where he tried to hide. He felt the pain and the heat as if he were back there.

He heard Daniel's breath catch and his friend stepped back from him. Paul opened his eyes and looked around. Streams of joy ran through grey. Some of that joy played in his friend. He turned his sight inward and saw the potential for joy, but also what was stopping it. He was still afraid. Though he didn't want the control of the Books, or the lies of the serpentines, he was afraid of letting go of himself to swim in the river of joy Daniel had found.

The Library called to him and he looked at the pictures. They flowed and moved. Animals played beside children. Fantastic creatures watched from the friendly shadows of the forest. Beings that were made of light danced and made the world brighter. Other creatures hung back on the edges of the dance both afraid and jealous of the dancers. They held Books in their hands between them and the light.

A hand landed on Paul's shoulder and he turned to look at who had interrupted him.

"Tag, Daniel," Paul said. "You're it!"

Daniel vanished from the sight of the guards that surrounded him.

"Where did he go?" one said.

"He was just here," the other said.

"It doesn't matter," the last one said. "We have the one we want."

Paul let the fire drop from his eyes and the head guard became just a guard again instead of a creature of fire and smoke. He followed the guards away toward the palace.

The palace was as immense as the back wall suggested. They didn't go in, as Paul expected, through the front door, but instead through a nondescript door in a side building. They pushed him into a room and closed the door behind him.

"Hello, Seerpharel," Paul said and leaned against the wall. "I heard that you flew away in panic from Arik."

"Beelphael wanted to come up and see how our plans in Rym were doing. Arik was going to be a waste of time for a while. Flying is so much faster than walking in the dust."

"So, how are your plans?"

"You seem to think that we are out to destroy the world," Seerpharel said, "but all we want is peace and order. Where would we be if all of you were gone? It would be boring. You are weak, but amusing." Paul allowed a little of the Sword's fire into his vision and looked at the serpentine. Her words were true, but not all the truth. The serpentine was mostly smoke with just the slightest hints of fire in her depths.

"You used to dance," Paul said.

"Fool," she said and Paul's vision returned to normal. He was looking at a petulant young woman. "We made those tools. They can't be used against us."

"Yet still, you used to dance."

"What good is dancing?" Seerpharel said. "It isn't my music. You understand, don't you?"

"Yes," Paul said, "I understand. It is hard to let go of my will to move to someone else's song."

"So you will join us," Seerpharel smiled. It was the same smile that he'd glimpsed through a door when she pulled Daniel into the room.

"Like I said, it is hard to let go of my will to move to someone else's music." Paul shook his head. "I don't think I could give myself to you anymore than you could give yourself to me."

"Then we will destroy you."

"I'm not sure you can," Paul said, "though you are welcome to try."

A sword of smoke and flame appeared in Seerpharel's hand. "I haven't done this in a while," she said, "but I am going to enjoy this." She leaped forward and ran the sword through Paul. He felt the pain, and heard the rock wall behind him burn, but he forced a smile on his face.

"I've faced the flame already," Paul said, "It showed me the truth of my fear. Shall I show you yours?" He called to the fire in him and blue flame twisted through the smoke. It crawled up toward Seerpharel's hands and she screamed.

A blast of power struck Paul and flung him through the wall, and the next and the one after that, then he was skidding through the square while paving stones burst into flames around him. People screamed and ran as a shooting star burst from the palace and curved high above him. A second star shot straight from the horizon and the two met, then vanished high into the air. Though it had only been seconds, the square was empty of life. No adult or child was in sight. Paul pushed himself to his feet and walked away toward the park where they were staying.

He found Daniel huddled in the shed.

"I thought they got you," Daniel said.

"They did."

"She was there."

"She was."

"How did you escape?"

"I dared her to destroy me." Paul took a deep breath and winced a little. "She didn't destroy me, but she did wreck a large part of the palace. Beelphael intercepted her before she could level the city, but I'm pretty sure they'll be back."

"We've got to go. We'll hide."

"You go," Paul said. "I'm not hiding. I'm going to go a little way north of here and wait for them to come."

"I can't just let you go by yourself."

"You must," Paul said. "I don't want you to get hurt."

"I'm your companion, Paul," Daniel said, "no matter what."

"Go, before it's too late. Go follow the children."

"It's already too late," Daniel said.

There was a bang on the side of the shed, then guards poured in with swords. They put the blades to Daniel's throat.

"He said we couldn't hurt you, but steel will cut your friend," the guard said. "Come with us or he dies."

Paul flicked his hand. The walls of the shed blew apart and guards flew out into the night. Except the one who was holding Daniel. Paul walked over and took the blade from him.

"Have you ever experienced pain?" Paul asked the serpentine guard. "You're so good at inflicting it, I'm sure you know what it feels like. Seerphael probably taught you." The guard didn't move. "You see, Daniel, he's trapped. He can't move. I learn quickly." He held the sword up to the guard's face. "I don't know if you've seen this before. The sword burst into blue flame. Paul could see the fear in the serpentine's eyes now. "I don't know if you can die, but maybe it's time I find out."

"No, Paul," Daniel said. He tried to pull Paul's arm away from the frozen guard. "You don't have to be this way. You don't have to be like them."

"But I am like them," Paul said, "I won't give myself up. I won't learn to play. He looked at the serpentine. "Just like this one wouldn't give himself to the dance. But don't worry, I'm not going to join them." He let his voice fill with flame. "I'm going to destroy them."

"Stop." Daniel was crying now. "You can't do this. You have a choice."

"Yes, Daniel," Paul said, "I have a choice. This is my choice."

"I can't stay," Daniel cried. "I can't. I can't watch you become this, this, evil!" He ran into the night.

Daniel's steps receded into silence as tears of blue fire ran down Paul's face.

Chapter 18

As Daniel fled into the dark horrible screams came from behind him. Great wrenching sobs forced their way out of him. After coming all this way to free themselves from the Book, Daniel had never imagined that the freedom they sought could become a choice for evil.

Blue flashes lit up the sky over Rym as Daniel ran toward the gate. The streets were empty of people. He might as well have been alone in the entire world. Daniel didn't know how long he ran before he collapsed. When he woke in the morning, there was a grey fog over everything. Stumbling his way through the city, he heard children laughing, but he didn't feel like playing.

Daniel found his way to the gate and slipped out with a group of people who were guiding a huge wagon full of lumber.

"Heading to Cepha," the driver said. "Book said they need lumber."

"I live near Cepha," Daniel said. "I could use a ride."

"Hop on. I could use the company."

The driver talked all the way to Cepha. He even talked in his sleep. Daniel didn't care. A vast numbness had taken over. It was like the fog had invaded his soul and turned everything grey.

"Nice riding with you," the driver said when he dropped Daniel in the market at Cepha. "You're good company."

Daniel stood in the market. It was early and no one was about. He walked straight through and headed south to Eben. A strange sensation inside his shirt made him stop. Daniel reached in and touched the Page he'd never given back to Paul. He pulled it out.

Play

Daniel shouted and tore the Page into shreds. He kept tearing until the Page drifted around him like red snow. When he was done, he walked on down the path toward his home.

It had taken him and Paul three days to walk from Eben to Cepha. It took Daniel four days to walk home. He wouldn't have made it if one of Zaccheus's servants hadn't found him lying on the path. The servant left his errand for Zaccheus and carried Daniel to the village.

Daniel woke in a strange bed. Diana was sitting in the chair watching him.

"How are you feeling?" she asked. The question had too many answers for Daniel, so he just let the tears run down his face. Diana dried his tears and brought him some broth with bread on the side. There was a dollop of honey on the bread. Daniel remembered how Paul talked about Diana's kiss tasting of honey. He wept again, and Diana fed him through his tears.

Daniel stayed in the bed for days before Diana could convince him to climb out and join her in the kitchen. Her father sat sleeping in a chair in the corner. Daniel listened to him snore while Diana went about the kitchen. She stirred the pot of broth and brushed breadcrumbs off the counter into her hand. She put them on the windowsill.

"The birds like them," she said.

The next day she served him bread and honey at the table. Her father ate his slowly, then went back to sleep.

"Where do you find your honey?" Daniel asked. "I only found honey once, just before we left."

"Come, I'll show you." Diana said. She took his hand and led him into the woods. The path looked oddly familiar though Daniel had never had any reason to travel this way.

"There," she said, "in the hollow tree." She pointed her finger and Daniel could see the cloud of bees buzzing.

"How did you find it?" Daniel asked.

"We used to come here all the time and get honey when we were children," Diana said. "Don't you remember?"

Daniel did remember, late in the evening, just before their parents would call. The bees would let them scoop a handful of honey to lick on the way home.

"You chose honey a lot in the game," Daniel said. He thought of a word lying on the path. He tickled Diana. "Tag, you're it," he shouted and ran off through the woods. At first he was clumsy and she almost caught him, but as he let the game take over he ducked and dodged through the trees. She finally caught him and tickled him until he laughed, then he laughed until he cried and she held him until the tears ended.

"Paul, isn't coming home," he said.

"I know."

"But Paul said that you kissed him so that he would come home again."

"That's just what the silly Book said. I knew he wasn't coming home. I heard him give everything he had to Zaccheus."

"But you kissed him anyway?"

"He was my friend too, before he forgot."

"I forgot too."

"You remember now?"

"Yes. Remember the day we rolled in the dirt?"

"Then we went swimming!" Diana jumped up. "Let's go swimming!" She pulled Daniel up and dragged him through the woods."

"How did you remember?" Daniel asked.

"I never forgot," Diana said. "I woke up that morning and the silly Book was there on my bed." She slowed down to let Daniel climb over a fallen tree. "I knew I was supposed to read the Book, Mom and Dad had talked about nothing else for days. I wanted some honey, so I left the Book where it was and went and got some. When I got home it was time for breakfast, so we ate breakfast. Dad showed me the cheese room and it sounded like a great game. I finally looked at the Book days later but it was just silly stuff. Do this, do that. It was all boring."

They reached the bank of the stream. Daniel recognised it immediately. Diana was squirming out of her clothes.

"Come on," she said. "Don't be slow."

"But…"

"It's no fun swimming with clothes on. Don't you remember?" She dropped her last piece of clothing and ran and jumped far out into the creek. Daniel remembered it was especially deep there. He threw his clothes off and made his own leap into the water. They splashed and played until their lips were blue.

"The silly Book said that I was supposed to marry Zaccheus's son," Diana said as they lay in the sun to dry. "But it was always you that I wanted to marry. I just said honey so not to make Paul jealous." She rolled over and kissed Daniel. Paul was right, she does taste like honey. Then he stopped thinking of anything but sunlight and warm bodies.

They swam again afterwards. As they came out of the water shivering and laughing, a child met them on the bank.

"Come with me," she said, and led them away to the east.

Chapter 19

As Daniel ran away, Paul turned to the serpentine trapped by his power.

"Imagine pain," he said through the fire of his tears and drew the sword along his arm. The blue fire was the worst pain he'd ever felt and he let a scream out into the night. The serpentine's eyes grew wide. "I was told that the truth hurts," Paul said, "but you have no idea." He ran the sword through his hand and another scream tore from his throat. Blue fire flashed into the sky. "I've even heard that the truth will set you free." Paul took the sword and ran himself through the heart. His scream was an explosion of blue flame and the serpentine was flung away into the air.

Paul pulled the sword from his chest and threw it away.

"Sorry, old friend," he said, "but it was time you went home." He watched the faint shooting star slow and shift course before streaking off to the east. When it had gone, he turned to the north and started walking. He wanted to be well away from the city before the serpentines came.

Fog descended on the city as he walked. Paul welcomed it. This wasn't a day for walking through the clear air. His heart ached, and not from the sword. Daniel had been with him through this whole journey. Even when he hadn't been in the same space as Paul, he was present close by, looking for him. This was the first time they were walking in opposite directions.

Even as he sorrowed, Paul was glad that Daniel hadn't remembered that the sword flamed for the lie, not the truth. The lie of driving Daniel away made the flame. That lie struck to his heart more than any blade. He reached the wall of the city and wrinkled his nose. Not far from where we left that wool merchant by the stench.

Paul left Rym by the simple expedient of walking through the wall leaving a smoking blue-tinged hole and his apologies behind him.

"We're being pretty hard on your city," he said, "but it would be worse if I stayed."

He walked north through fields of wildflowers. The path took him past a couple of villages, but not close enough to see the people.

Paul didn't know how long it took him to reach the mountains. He walked far into the range before finally stopping on a wide sloping rock plain. This would do. Sitting in the middle of the plain, he sent a thin blue beam of light up into the heavens.

The shooting stars came from every point in the sky as if all the stars actually did fall to earth. They came directly at him. There was no subtlety, no arguments. The serpentines weren't coming to coerce him into joining them. Paul had threatened them, now they were going to destroy him. Unless he destroyed them first.

The force of the serpentines landing melted the rock. An army of flame and smoke, they surrounded and hung over him above.

"You have challenged me," Beelphael called down from the heavens, "and I will crush you for your impudence."

"Are there not others more powerful than you?" Paul said.

"Not in this place," Beelphael replied and the attack began. Fire and smoke surrounded Paul and swords cut at his flesh. Pieces of himself fell away. No matter how brightly he made the blue fire burn, he couldn't touch enough of them. He was losing himself. Paul remembered the children and adults in the market; occupying the same place but living in different worlds. He called up the memory of that game, and instead of filling himself with the blue fire, he became fire.

Paul began to dance. He was awkward and ridiculous; sure that if the serpentines weren't trying to cut him to pieces, they would have laughed at him. He laughed at himself. What had Daniel said? Give yourself over to the game, the dance. Paul stopped thinking and just became the dance. The serpentines who tried to follow him had to fit themselves into the steps. Beings that had refused to dance to any tune for aeons found themselves dancing with blue fire. Their smoke wafted away and their flames burned clean and white. They surprised themselves with song. Others felt the rhythm of the steps, and fled in fear.

Finally only Beelphael, Seerpharel and Paul were left standing on the ruined plain. The music of transformed serpentines still hung in the air.

"You will not destroy us."

"I know."

"Nor will we be transformed."

"No," Paul said, "Even you have a choice. Your fault was that you tried to take the choice of others away."

"We tried to make this world a better place."

"For who?" Paul said. "Not for us, not for people trapped in fear of God."

"You would have failed. You would have angered God, and He would have destroyed this place."

"God will not destroy this world."

"How can you know!" Beelphael's voice rang with fear.

"If I will endure such pain to preserve my friend, what will God endure to save the world?"

"We have made it so the world doesn't need saving."

"No," Paul said, "you have made a world without joy."

"Safety is better than joy."

"Is it?" Paul asked and smiled.

Beelphael and Seerpharel looked east suddenly.

"What have you done?" they cried then leaped into the air.

Paul followed them; a blue streak after red across the sky.

They landed in front of a gap in a tall hedge. A child was leading Daniel and Diana to the Garden.

"Stop," the serpentines said. "You may not pass."

"This isn't your Garden," Daniel said. "You have no power to stop us."

The serpentines formed a wall of flame and smoke, but the child just walked through and Daniel and Diana followed.

"You have doomed us all!" the serpentines wailed and fled across the sky.

Paul followed Daniel and Diana into the Garden. It was truly a marvelous place. The paintings on the library barely hinted at its beauty. Paul's friends were standing in front of a marvelous tree.

"Here is the Tree of the Knowledge of Good and Evil," the child said. "Its Fruit will set all your people free of the Books. They will be able to choose joy for themselves."

"Or evil," Daniel said sadly.

"Just taste it and be free."

"Free of what?"

"Free to choose Good or Evil for yourselves."

Diana reached out and picked a fruit from the tree.

Daniel took it from her and looked at it for a long time.

"In the story," he said finally, "it is the serpent who tries to convince the man and the woman to eat the fruit in disobedience of God. The serpentines are afraid of what we might do here, but you aren't, are you?"

"You have the power to shake the heavens to its foundations," the child said.

"What," Daniel said, "if I don't want to shake the heavens? If I want to go home and raise chickens and have a family? What if I don't want to choose between Good and Evil." He turned his hand over and let the fruit fall to the ground. "I want to choose Joy." He looked at Diana and smiled. "What do I need beyond that?"

"Fool," the child said, "There will be others after you. Someone will eat the Fruit."

"And what of it?" asked Daniel. "That will be their choice then. I can only choose what I choose."

"Adam in the Garden,
so very sad is he,
scared to pick the apple
from God's Tree." Diana chanted.
"Eve in the evening
weeping in the night,
afraid she'll get God angry

if she takes a bite." Daniel said.
"What makes God happy?
What makes God sad?
Be foolish or wise
But choose you must!" they said together.

"You," Daniel said looking at her.

"You," Diana said looking at him.

"You are pathetic," the child said and stomped off into the woods.

"So, Paul," Daniel said, "is this what you wanted?"

"Is it what you wanted?" Paul asked as he walked to his friend.

"Yes," Daniel said, "it is."

"Good," Paul said.

"Do you think God is pleased?"

"What did God say to the man and the woman?" Paul asked.

"Prosper and enjoy life."

"I think God is well pleased."

"She hasn't left us?" Diana asked?

"No, she never will," Paul said. "It's time to go home. Follow me if you can." He ran off into the Garden with Daniel and Diana chasing him. Within minutes they were back at the pool in the creek.

"I didn't know the Garden was so close," Diana said.

"I think it's even closer than that," Daniel said, and pulled her close for a kiss.

"Dad will be waiting for his supper," she said after a bit.

They got dressed and walked away through the woods hand in hand.

"Good job," God said.

"Thanks," Paul said, "since I seem to have given my garden away, may I go and putter around in yours?"

"Of course," God said, "you're always welcome there."

She looked out over the world. Children played while adults walked blindly. But in a tiny village a man put down his bundle of sticks to play tag with his son. In another village across the world, a mother chanted and clapped with her baby on her knee.

"What makes God happy?

What makes God sad?

Be foolish or wise

But choose you must!" the mother said to her baby.

"You," God said, "I choose you. All of you."

Acknowledgements

By The Book is the result of my first Three Day Novel competition. The story had been growling in my head for a while, but it took trying to write a novel in seventy-two hours to get it on paper. The Three Day Novel is now a regular occurrence in out house hold.

Writing the novel is only the first step, and I have to thank my editor Dean C. Moore for his work to get the polishing done. After that I have to thank the betas who also gave input on how it worked and where I should go with the story. Diane Jortner was particularly helpful in that regard.

I can't write a novel without mentioning my wife and muse, Alexandra Béasse who made me read the books I write out loud to her and thus helps me find all the issues I would otherwise miss.

About the author

Alex is a writer, reviewer and editor and makes his living talking. It's clear that he loves words. Since the first he started writing stories, to this novel, words have kept him mostly sane. He lives in Flin Flon which is thick with writers and he's fortunate to be able to share with them both his stories and theirs.

He has three dogs who contest the space under his desk a little more aggressively than his feet would like. This may explain some of the errors in his typing. Yet the company of them breathing while he works late at night is something he cherishes.

By The Book is Alex's third novel. His other novels, The Unenchanted Princess and Playing on Yggdrasil are available at Smashwords and Amazon as well as other e-book retailers.

For more information or to contact Alex, check out http://alexmcgilvery.com

Illustrator

Danita Stallard started telling stories at a young age, and never grew up enough to stop. Her love of cartooning, calligraphy, and fantastical storytelling has inspired her to delve into the world of graphic novels, so when she isn't pursuing the life of an author, she can likely be found amidst sketchpads and eraser crumbs.

Stallard's online portfolio can be found at:
www.flittermouse.weebly.com

Sample of Playing on Yggradrasil

Prologue

"No Father wants to lose a child," the preacher said. "In First Peter, we hear the faithful told to be patient as God does not want anyone to be lost."

Too late, Patrick thought. He tried to look away from the box that held all that was left of Ingrid. Justine held his hand and leaned her head on his arm. He was all that Justine had now. He needed to be strong for her. He hadn't been strong enough for Ingrid and now she was gone. Lost, in spite of what Pastor Daniel was saying.

There was a rustle as the people in the church all stood and Patrick saw the funeral director waiting for him and his daughter to lead everyone out of the church.

At the cemetery they put the obscenely small box of his wife's ashes in the hole. He threw a handful of dirt in after it and the tears pricked at his eyes. He forced them back with an iron will. He was not going to cry in front of his daughter.

"Is Mommy in that box?" Justine asked looking at him with her blue eyes.

"No." Patrick had to stop and take a deep breath. "No, Justine, that's just what is left of her. She's out there somewhere."

"Is she lost? Can we help her come home?"

"She isn't lost. Nothing we really love is ever lost." Patrick had to take another breath and push back the tears. He could feel the weakness trying to claw its way out. He wanted to howl and tear his clothes.

"She can't come home," Patrick said, "She's with God."

He felt a bitter acid in his stomach at the G word. It was a cop-out, but Ingrid had given an ironclad faith in the big guy to Justine. He wondered what he really believed. All he knew was that there was a jagged hole in his life that no amount of words were ever going to fill.

"Say hi to God for me, Mommy." Justine threw some dirt into the hole, then brushed her hands off. "I'm going to talk to Molly, OK Dad?"

"OK," Patrick said. He watched her run off. Her blond hair streamed out behind her. He wanted to call her back and hold on to her and make sure that she was safe. Instead he looked back at the hole. "You can fill it in now," he told the funeral director. She just nodded and a man in overalls quietly shovelled the dirt into the grave. It didn't take long. Patrick wanted to let the tears flow, but the traitorous weakness mocked him by keeping his eyes as dry as the dirt covering his wife and lover's grave.

It should be raining, he thought. The heavens should have opened and the whole world should be deluged. Let the clouds weep the tears that he couldn't. He heard the squeals of Justine and Molly playing. He envied them at the same time that he felt bereft of company.

"If you need anything, just call." The minister handed him yet another card. Patrick was sure he had twenty of them lying around the house.

"Give one to Justine," he said. Then he thought how ungracious he sounded. "Thanks for all your help."

"I heard what you told Justine," Reverend Daniel said, "about nothing loved ever being lost. Remember that." He patted Patrick's shoulder and ambled off toward Justine. Patrick watched him kneel in the grass to talk to her. She took the card and ran arrow straight back to Patrick.

"Can we go home?" she asked.

"Sure thing, Justine."

They walked back to the limousine he'd rented, not certain of his ability to drive, not wanting to put anyone else at risk. The driver was leaning against the door waiting for them. He didn't say anything, but opened the door for Justine and closed it behind Patrick.

The ride home was lost in the fog of grief that threatened to overwhelm Patrick. Justine sat beside him and chattered about the service and the other people who were there. The fog followed him into the house. He couldn't remember talking to people, though he was sure he must have said something in response to their endless words of sorrow and support.

"Justine wanted spaghetti," Patrick's sister was saying to him. "So I made her some. It's ready if you would like some." Patrick thought of the awful void inside him. No amount of spaghetti would ever fill it.

"Sure, thanks." He was aware that she was shepherding the last of the people out the door before she went out herself. He followed the garlic and tomato smell to the kitchen as if he could get lost in his own house. Yet he felt lost.

"Hi, Daddy," Justine said, "you need to eat something." She was echoing what she had heard every other woman in the house tell him. She pulled him into a chair and climbed into his lap. She whispered in his ear, as if her words were the secret of the universe. "I know Mommy's with God, but I'm still sad. The minister said it was OK to cry. Is it?"

Patrick looked into his daughter's eyes and saw the same dry pain that he knew was in his.

"Yes," he said, "it's OK to cry." The floodgates opened and he saw her tears as he felt his. Then she clung to him with all the strength of her eight-year-old arms. He felt her wet face against his and their tears and their grief and their love mixed.

"I'll always be there for you." Patrick whispered into the blond hair. "Always."

*119599191*C